GLIMPSE

CAROL LYNCH WILLIAMS

WITHDRAWN

A PAULA WISEMAN BOOK

Simon & Schuster BFYR

New York London Toronto Sydney

Simon & Schuster BFYR

An imprint of Simon & Schuster Children's Publishing Division
1230 Avenue of the Americas, New York, New York 10020

Simon & Schuster BFYR

is a trademark of Simon & Schuster, Inc.

For information about special discounts for bulk purchases, please contact Simon &
Schuster Special Sales at 1-866-506-1949 or business@simonandschuster.com.
The Simon & Schuster Speakers Bureau can bring authors to your live event. For more
information or to book an event, contact the Simon & Schuster Speakers Bureau at
1-866-248-3049 or visit our website at www.simonspeakers.com.

Book design by Lizzy Bromley
The text for this book is set in Gill Sans and Strangelove.
Manufactured in the United States of America

2 4 6 8 10 9 7 5 3 1

Library of Congress Cataloging-in-Publication Data
Williams, Carol Lynch.
Glimpse / Carol Lynch Williams.
p. cm.
"A Paula Wiseman book."
Summary: Living with their mother who earns money as a prostitute, two sisters take
care of each other and when the older one attempts suicide, the younger one tries to
uncover the reason.
ISBN 978-1-4169-9730-6 (hardcover : alk. paper)
[1. Novels in verse. 2. Sisters—Fiction. 3. Mothers and daughters—Fiction.
4. Suicide—Fiction. 5. Sexual abuse—Fiction.] I. Title.
PZ7.5.W55Gl 2010
[Fic]—dc22
2009041147
ISBN 978-1-4169-9732-0 (eBook)

FIRST EDITION

FOR

my favorite daughters
(you know who you are)

AND

all the world's Lizzies

1.

In one moment
it is over.
In one moment
it is gone.
The morning grows
thin, gray

and our lives—
how they were—
have vanished.
Our lives have
changed

when I walk
in on Lizzie
my sister
holding a shotgun.

She fingers the
trigger.

Looks up.
My sister.
My sister just looks
up at me.

Touching
the trigger

of that gun.

2.

My breath goes,
lungs empty,
all the blood
runs up to my face.
My heart pounds so
that it hurts.
It hurts.

What are you doing,
Lizzie girl?
I say,
sounding just like Momma,
only not so loud.
The words are
without air
full of blood
and pain.

What are you doing?
I'm on one knee now
face-to-face
with Lizzie.

Just thinking,
she says.

Momma?
I say over my shoulder.
Momma!

And to Lizzie,
What are you thinking?
I'm not even sure
I can hear her answer,
the blood pounds
so in my ears.

Just thinking,
Lizzie says,
looking me right in the eye,
just thinking about

leaving.

3.

Wait—back up.
Back up and see the story
of Momma, Lizzie, and
me.

Of Lizzie and
me
and how the two
of us
got here

to this moment.

4.

Mama she say, Shh.
She say, Shhh.
She say, Quiet, baby.

5.

I love babies,
Momma says.
I love babies most of all.

6.

In the beginning
it was me
and Liz
and Momma
and Daddy.

The four of us.
Together.
Me and Liz just
babies.

Smiling, no teeth. Bottles.
Saggy diapers.
Sunburned cheeks.

All those old
pictures
Momma has hidden
under her
bed in that
box,
all those
pictures prove
we were a family
before.

7.

He left me,
Momma used to say
(and sometimes does
still
now),
when it was late
and she
felt lighter
from Pabst Blue Ribbon
and the hour.

He left *me*.
She thumped her chest,
tears making her eyes glisten.

Me and Liz
were quiet
on the edge
of the living room
watching
looking
listening.
Even from this far
away
I could see

the tears
in Momma's eyes

Me and Liz
we sat quiet.
We stayed
we listened
because we had to.

The more she drank,
raising can after can,
the more Momma talked
and soon
would let out the truth.

She let out the truth
and the reason me and Liz
were still in the room,
like she always does.

He left me,
Momma said,
because I had
two kids.

Then she cried right out loud.

And I couldn't help it.
I cried
with her.
Lizzie patting my shoulder.

Shhh,
Lizzie said.
Shhh.

You were his kids
too,
Momma said.

I cried along with her,
till she fell asleep, quiet, on the sofa
and Lizzie would say,
Hope, it's time for bed.

8.

Once
after Daddy left
on his bike
and didn't come back

Miss Freeman
waddled her way across
the street and
over to our place
with a big platter of fried catfish
and hush puppies and
a dish of potatoes and
a salad.

For you, Ms. Chapman,
she said.
I heared what happened
and I thought
you could use some good
Southern cooking.

Momma cried in Miss Freeman's arms
and me and Lizzie
ate all the hush puppies before

Momma had dried her
eyes.

Looks like you girls
need some more of them
things,
Miss Freeman said.
And she brought us a whole
bowlful more.

9.

Miss Freeman
taught me
and Lizzie to play
rummy
and Chinese checkers
and let us watch
Wheel of Fortune
at her place
on the nights
Momma worked.

And when Momma
tried to pay her,
Miss Freeman said,
Ms. Chapman, I love these girls
like they was my own.

She laid a heavy hand
on my head
and I felt the pressure
of that hand
long after I had gone to bed.

14

10.

Lizzie was my job.
And I was hers.

It is your job,
Momma said
to us years ago
when me and Liz
came home from school
one day.
(Almost six
and
seven
years old.)

We were late,
late coming home from
the bus.
Playing in the
huge puddle of
mud and
water
there
in the dirt road.

Didn't notice the time passing.

15

Till Miss Freeman—
old as the sun—
hollered out,
You girls know
what time it is?
Your momma is gonna be worried sick
about you two
playing in the road.

We move when we
see cars,
Lizzie said.

She had mud all over,
splashed on her
face even.
I was soaked through too.

I know it,
Miss Freeman said.
Git on home.

We got.

Momma, though,

she was even later
coming in that night,
not waiting for us
at all.

Lizzie and me
we changed our clothes,
dried the dirty places
off our legs
on a towel,
and waited.

We watched us some TV,
turned up real loud,
and waited
some more on the sofa.

And when the sun was set
coloring the sky a thin
line of hibiscus red,
Momma pulled into the
drive.

Both me and Liz,
we looked at each other,

and I felt so glad that Momma had
made it home.
I let out a breath
I'd been holding all afternoon.

Now we could
eat
and not be afraid
or worried
that she
might leave
like Daddy did.
Might not come back
at all.

You make any dinner?
Momma asked Lizzie
while looking through
the fridge.

No,
Lizzie said.

Momma's lips made a line
—like a dash—

and she said,
I got me a new job.
Then she smiled.
A good job.
It'll take time,
this job. I'll be
busier.

Momma walked over to us,
smoothed my hair,
patted on Lizzie's shoulder.
We're gonna have us some money.
More than now.

She squatted down till I could see,
in her eyes,
a bit of me
and a bit of Liz
and the light
from the fridge.

I'll be working more and more,
she said.
And I expect you two
to help out around here.

Lizzie nodded.
Okay, Momma,
she said.
And I said,
Okay, Momma,
too.

Momma thought.

Then she said,
It is your job,
Liz,
to take care of your
little sister.

And you, Hope,
Momma said
her finger pointing like
she meant it,
you take care of Lizzie.

You hear me?

I nodded. So did
Lizzie.

Then we grinned at each
other,
showing our teeth.

All right then,
Momma said.
We are a team.
The Chapman Girls'
team.
Let's go get us some
McDonald's
for dinner
'cause I got money.

And she waved two twenties in the air.

I was so glad
she was home
and safe
and we were headed
to McDonald's,
a team.

11.

Daddy,
I know,
did not mean
to leave us—
though
Momma sometimes
sees it was
me
and Liz
that sent him away.

He was coming
home
to all
of
us,
bringing
cough syrup for Lizzie
from the Piggly Wiggly,
when
he got himself
killed on that
motorcycle
of his.

Damn motorcycle,
Momma
said.
Damn cough that
Lizzie had.
Damn
damn
damn.

And I agree.

12.

It's my job now
(like it was then
when we were
almost six and seven),
I know it,
to make Lizzie
happy.

No matter that I am
younger,
that I am
almost thirteen and she's
fourteen.

The two of us
work hard
for
the two of us.

And have
since
the olden days,
with Momma
changing
more and more

as time passed
and it became clear
that all the praying
she did
would never bring
her dead husband back

and all the praying
in the world
me and Lizzie did
wouldn't keep
Momma from falling
in her own work
and away from us

more and more.

13.

So we grow up alone
without Daddy
with Miss Freeman
looking in on us
from time to time
with Momma busy
more and more.

Me and Lizzie.
Together.

Until it all begins
with that
gun.

14.

Last night
me and Lizzie
sit
in the dark,
sit on my bed,
in the quiet of
night.

We're all grown up,
I think.

But we are
having us some
troubles.

Now all I can hear is
our breathing,
and from outside,
the frogs and crickets
singing nighttime songs.

I can see the shadow shape of
trees. A light wind
moves the leaves
like a waving hand.

I talk soft at the
side of Lizzie's head.

Right now I
think of her like the tiny baby she was,
drinking green Kool-Aid
from a bottle,
biting the nipple so
it hung from her mouth,
and slapped her
baby chest.

The picture tucked under
the bed with
the rest—

the picture that proves
a father
a mother
and two sisters.

My own bottle of Kool-Aid.
Me on my back.
Feet supporting that
bottle.

(And Momma laughing.
Laughing!)

I say to Liz on this night,
I say,
'Member last night how
I was upset at you
'cause you couldn't sleep?

Liz nods.
She stares off
away
like she sees past the walls
of our
room.

I smell VO5 shampoo
in her hair,
balsam flavor.

'Member I told you,
I say,
to get on out of our room
if you wouldn't be quiet?

She cried long into the night.
Has been
weeping
for days now.
Crying when the sun
settles to rest itself
past the lip of the world.
Even in her sleep,
crying.

I was just tired then,
I say.
Thinking of that
baby
picture.
Thinking of the
Before
photos and what
they prove.

'Member afterwards I snuggled
you up,
I say,
and then we went to sleep?

Again Liz nods.

Good,
I say,
I just want you
to remember.

And *I* remember,
I remember,
how I promised
before
to take care of
Lizzie
who is not
as strong as me.

Momma says so.

15.

And then
this morning—
all bright for a minute—
turns dark on me
turns in on me
when
I walk into
the bathroom and
see my sister
fingering the
trigger
of the
shotgun
Momma uses to kill
pygmy rattlers
when we go
to the lake.

Lizzie looks at me
her finger just touching that
trigger
and I say,

What are you doing, Lizzie girl?
I sound just like Momma,
only not so loud.
What are you doing?

16.

I can't see it right.
I can't see it clear.

Did I do this wrong?

17.

She's
fourteen
and
has tried to kill herself.

I cannot see it.
I cannot see the why.

Why?
Momma says,
loud in Liz's face.

We stand in the living room
all of us,
with that bright
sun splashing
on the floor at
our feet,
waiting for the police
to carry my sister
away.

I didn't shoot,
Lizzie says.

But Momma's called the cops
anyway.

(It is my responsibility
to take care of
Liz.)

I won't do this,
Momma says. I won't do this.
I won't lose
anyone
not even
one
more
time.

(And Liz's
supposed to take care of
me.)
Liz,
my Lizzie,
she does not answer.
But she does look
at Momma.

She looks at her
so hard
so long
that Momma
finally turns away.

18.

I am old with living.
So much older than almost thirteen.

And things aren't right.
Not at all.

Is Lizzie nuts
like Momma says?
(It runs in the family,
you know?
No, Momma, I
didn't know.)

Is Momma?

Is it me who is crazy,
twisted tight with all of this?
So tight
I am not sure I can
breathe.

There's been
a spiral in time,
things changing so
fast

I don't know my sister
anymore.

Oh, Liz.
Stop that thinking so you can
come back.

19.

Before all this,
before Liz grew
weary of living

we used to laugh.

Once,
Momma
put me and Liz
in the car
and said,
We are going
garage sale-ing
and you can get yourselves
whatever you want.

Me and Liz,
we whooped it up!
Laughed out loud.

Momma flung us
some money to the backseat.
Lots of ones,
folded so many times

40

they were soft
as an old blanket.

We rode up and
down the streets
of Ormond,
passed the 7-Eleven,
passed the Piggly Wiggly
looking for signs.

All around us
the smell of pine
and the salt of the ocean,
the clatter of palm fronds
when the wind pushed through,
cooling the air
for us.

There's one,
I'd say.
There's one,
Lizzie would say.

And Momma,
she would throw

her head back
and laugh.
Then
help us dig
through boxes of
toys,
the hot sun simmering,
to find just the right thing,
just the thing
me
or Lizzie
had been hoping
for.

20.

That very afternoon
of the gun day,
Momma and me
stand at the edge of a parking lot,
the end-of-school
weather throbbing
around us,
hot.

Oaks dip toward the ground,
lining the lawn
shading the sidewalk.
This grass is like carpet.

I cannot recall the time we step in
the hospital
but
it's chilly in the building,
dark
after outside.
A
goose runs over
my grave.

Don't think that.

43

This way,
Momma says,
and walks right past
the front desk like
she knows this hospital.

No one questions her.
No one stops us.

Somehow
we sneak down one hall
then another
and another,
in the green coolness of
the hospital,
until we
stand in
a corridor
with a sofa that has no back.

Momma holds an unlit cigarette
to her lips.
Shhh, she says, shhh.
I nod.

Down some,
there's a huge door,
pale green.
The sign,
printed in block letters,
black letters:

LOCKDOWN UNIT

I can see it
from where I sit
and I shiver
again.

Up high
in the door
is a window,
big enough for just eyes
to look through.

And there is wire inside the glass.

Who can get through there?
I say to Momma,

nodding to that
window.
Can't no one squeeze through
that little rectangle.

But she doesn't answer.
Just waves her cigarette at me
and chews at her nails
that bleed from
torn cuticles.

I am
scared and
sick
so that I might throw up.

I sit on the edge of my seat,
try to catch just a glimpse
of that huge door
by looking at things through one
squinted eye.

With one eye
the sign looks even
farther away.

LOCKDOWN UNIT

My momma,
out of nowhere,
she sobs.

But I don't shed a tear.
I am the strong one.

Then I hear them from down the hall.
Coming our way.

And

there is Liz
caught
between two men.
One on each side.
Their hands tight
on her arms.

She
fights.

My sister the fighter,

who almost gave up
to try and kill herself,
she
slings her body this way and that.

I stand
to go to her.
To get to her.
To take care of her.
But Momma, she grabs at my arm,
pinching.

There's an
animal in my throat
that wants to scream
its way out.

It could tear my
throat apart,
I think.

They get to the door
to the sign
Liz fightingfightingfighting.
One guy

he presses at a buzzer
I somehow missed
seeing.

Liz works
to free herself.
Growling.

Oh baby,
Momma says.
Her voice is a long wail,
twisting like a snake.

Liz turns and looks back.

She catches sight of us.
Me one step closer.
Momma holding on to my arm.

Now Liz screams.
Now she bucks.
Now she throws her body
from side to side:
a wild thing.

My guts wrench for Liz.
They tie themselves
into a knot.

I take another step
but Momma
pulls me back.

Don't let them take me,
Hope,
Liz says,
don't let them take me.

Her voice
pierces me in the chest,
right under
the breastbone.

And my heart,
right then and there,
rips in half.
I can feel the weepy
tear in it.

One man says,

How the hell
did the two of them get up
here? Call
security.

Now Momma cries loud,
banging her fists on the wall,
dropping her head
like it is too
heavy to hold
up
on that skinny neck of hers.

I've never seen her act this way before.

My Liz, she fights
and hollers
and begs.
No time for anyone to call
with Lizzie fighting
like that.

Hope,
Lizzie says
my name over

and
over
and
over
again.
Hope!

And, oh,
I stand there.

Oh, my heart.

I stand there,
still.

Get her inside,
the man says.
He looks at Momma
crying,
wailing,
and at me,
unmoving,
and says,
Get the hell out of

here.
This is a restricted
area.
His voice is loud as Liz's.

The door opens
and then
Liz is
gone
from us.

But not before she
calls out.
One last time.
My sister says,
Hope.

My name echoes in the hall
long after
that door is closed.

21.

I need words
for what has happened
here
and there aren't any.
Not for what I have seen.

At first
I sit, quiet,
on the sofa with
no back.
Then I get up
and walk myself over
to that heavy door
and
tap
on
it.

My hand shakes.

I press my ear
to the metal,
all cold.

Lizzie?

22.

I want to talk
but no voice
comes out.

And that door
stays shut
tight.

Don't be so
damn melodramatic,
Momma says
and gives a sniff,
wiping at her nose with her arm.

Then she is crying again.
Without tears.
Lighting up
her cigarette
right there in the
hospital.

After a while,
when I think I can make it,
I lead Momma

to the elevator,
holding her up.

Outside the sun
is so bright
it feels like noon
but I know
it can't be,
that it's way
later in the day
than that.

Momma stumbles off
the sidewalk,
almost falling to one knee.
And I throw back
my head
and laugh like nothing
else.

The thing is,
though,
I don't think
it is a bit
funny.

23.

All these years,
Momma says, driving us
up the coast
toward home,
following the old
beach highway.

All these years,
she says,
I kept us
from government help.

Until now.

The hospital and Lizzie are behind us.

Ormond and welfare wait for us
up the road some.

It's growing dark,
the sky turning
pink and gold
with just that much blue.

Momma is quiet

smoking
smoking
her eyes dripping
like she has leaks.

Then she says,
Your daddy and me
used to drive
this old road on his bike.

You did?
I say.
I never knew.

There's lots you don't know,
Momma says.

And she is right about
that.

She is right
about
that.

24.

Momma:

1. Applies for welfare.

2. Hollers at my absent daddy.

3. Settles down for a few drinks.

I:

1. Sneak out of the house.

2. Grab my bike from the falling-down
   garage.

3. Pedal on over to Mari's.

I pedal as
fast as
I can.

Quiet past Miss Freeman's place
past the trailer park,

gripping
the handlebars,
past the
library.

Mouth open wide,
a scream so loud
my eyes squinch shut.

A scream for Lizzie
who I was supposed to
take care of.

25.

In a whisper of words
I can say
that Mari
is my best friend
second only to
my sister.
Has been
since third grade.
Will be
until
the two of us
die.

26.

Bicycling along,
screaming,
helps.
Makes some of the
pain
go away.

The rest slips
into my feet
as I
steer across
the grass
of Mari's front yard.

I drop the bike
near the petunias
and go to
knock
but Mari
slings the door wide
and shouts,
What took you so
damn long to
get here?

Then she laughs
big and I can
see her molars.
She doesn't have
even one cavity.

She wears an old
AFI T-shirt
and her hair
is purple today.

I matched it
to the petunias,
Mari says,
when I raise my eyebrows
at her.

Almost,
I say.
Almost that color
exactly.

Come on in here,
Mari says.

I breathe deep
the smell of air-conditioning
and flowers,
and step into the
house.

27.

Mari's momma and daddy
own the local
greenhouse called
Plants Are People Too.

Long buildings,
full of seedlings in early spring,
spindly weedy-looking
almost-plants a few weeks
later,
then tables full of color,
is their job.

Sometimes
I help
pressing seeds into
the moist dirt
or pulling sprouted
weeds that grow faster
than marigolds and
petunias
or going to the greenhouses
late, late, late
with Mari and her
daddy to make sure

the pipes haven't frozen
in the winter.

Sometimes
I play games with her family—
like with Miss Freeman—
or eat dinner cooked by Mari's momma
at the table with them all
(not brought in from
McDonald's or Burger King)
served from a platter
shaped liked roses.

And sometimes
I pretend Mari's momma
and daddy
are *my* momma
and daddy
though I have
never told anyone that,
not even Liz.

Now, they nod hello
when I come inside,

my scream ringing
in my ears,
and hold Mattie
(Mari's little sister)
tight
so
me and Mari can have
us some time talking
alone.

I don't say a word
not one word
about
Liz.

Mari knows what's happened.
I told her on the phone.
That's the best
I can do
right now.

28.

My momma.
My
momma,

she gets paid
for her time with
men.

She folds the money,
sometimes
tens
and twenties,
sometimes
lots of ones and
once a fifty,
and puts it into her bra for
safekeeping.

I keep it quiet,
and so did Liz,
when she was here.

This is a secret
I didn't know

I should be ashamed of
until a few years ago.

Shame
makes a person
keep their lips pressed
tight together.
I know.

Never tell no one,
Momma says.
And I
don't.

Momma hasn't
always done jobs
like this.

She used
to work at the
Piggly Wiggly,

but she got fired for coming in
a little drunk.

She had lots of jobs—
working the counter at McDonald's,
selling Avon,
even calling people for hair
appointments

none were her favorite

or made this kind of money,
Momma says.

She would never
work with flowers.
Not petunias
or asters
or climbing roses trained to a trellis.
She's said so.

29.

It was
right there—
when Momma
last worked at
the Piggly Wiggly—
that I saw a magazine
and Ian St. Clair
on the cover.

He sings on the radio.
Songs that make
my eyes tear up.

I think I love him.

30.

I have
three dreams
for myself.

One
is to be a writer,
telling stories
about true life and
maybe about
aliens.

Two.
Be a country and western singer
if I don't get rich
writing books.

(Momma and me and Lizzie
we practiced
before Liz left, practiced
singing.

Liz or me lead or alto.
Momma tenor.)

Three.
My third dream
is to kiss Ian St. Clair
right on the lips.
(Maybe
we would sing onstage
together.)

Could be
any one of these dreams
is possible,
so I keep on hoping.

No one
knows
this brand-new plan
I'm just coming up with
but Mari.

I'd never tell
Momma
and I can't tell
Liz

until
she comes
back.

31.

Out behind the house,
in a field
where only one cow lives,
Momma tells me
to throw the dead cats.

It's six days since
Lizzie's gone,
though it seems a forever,
and now this.

They're kittens, really.
A momma cat wandered up,
had them here,
then one day
just didn't come back.

A momma don't often
leave her babies,
Momma said to me and
Lizzie
when this happened.

Now, these babies?
They cry out to me before they die.

One by one.
The whole
litter almost gone.

I use an old rake
to pick the dead cats up
and sling their weight
far from me.

It is hot,
last days of May hot,
the air so heavy
breathing
is like drinking,
just about.

Don't
think
about
any
of
it.

All at once

I am mad at Liz!
White-hot
mad!

Why did you do it?
I yell at her,
clenching my fists
so tight
and looking toward where the bodies
are hidden
in the high grasses
on the far
side of the
fence.

Why did you
try to leave me,
Liz?

I'm on my knees,
shovel
beside me.

All these babies
dying

and I don't know why.

Just like with
my Lizzie.

I don't know

why.

32.

In the morning
two kittens are left.
The small black and white one
will be the next to go.
I know.
I can tell.

It lays on its side
near the kitchen door.
I crouch close,
pushing my hair
behind one ear
when it falls in my face.

Little one,
I say.
And I think,
Not a thing I can do for you.

(Like Liz.)

There's a place
in my heart that
I make thick

when I look at this
baby.

My old heart,
feeling fifty.
Feeling a hundred and fifty.
Or a million and fifty.

Lizzie,
Lizzie,
Lizzie
runs through my head.

Throw 'em
over the fence
once they're dead,
Momma said,
wiping tears
from her cheeks,
when I told her
they were all dying.

Don't pester me no more.
They're strays. And

I got me a friend
coming by.
I need time to get ready.

Fixing herself up all shiny,
all pretty,
wiping at the
tears.
I could see
lots of her there in the
mirrors.
My momma
so pretty.

I got me a friend coming over
and
I don't want no trouble
from you.
Hightail it outta here.

So I watch
that black and white kitten
knowing
I will have to throw

another body into
the high weeds.

Lizzie,
Lizzie,
Lizzie,
I say.

I sit outside on the
concrete steps
thinking of my sister
and all these kittens,
gone.

33.

Late that afternoon,
when the last
kitten is dead,
I bike my way to Mari's house.

I am hollow inside
from it all.

Look at this camera,
Mari says, when I walk
in her room,
clicking my picture before
I even have a chance
to smile.

My father bought it
for me.

She snaps another picture and
another
and one more.
And I almost
forget
every
awful

thing
in
my
life.

Stop it!
I want to say, but
I'm laughing.

We can do something
with these,
she says.
Maybe I can blackmail
you.

But first,
she says aiming the camera,
more
pictures.

I pose,
hand on my head,
covering my mouth,
pointing to my butt.

Mari poses,
pulling at her hair,
mouth wide open,
grabbing her bosoms.

We take pictures,
laughing the whole
time.
Carrying on
till Mari's mother
stops in to see what's going on.

We're leaping on Mari's bed,
both of us, leaping,
catching action shots.

What are you two doing?
her mother says
just as the bed collapses.

I hit the floor
on both knees,
and roll onto my back.

Mari falls to the floor, purple
hair every-which-way.
She aims the camera.
I point to my O-shaped
mouth.

Snap!

34.

Enough of Ian St. Clair,
Mari says a few days
after the kittens,
after the photos,
after we have gone
through three magazines
full of the singer.
He's hot and all,
but what about Robbie
or Spencer or Jeff?
Boys that live close.
What about Jace?

Jace Nelson?
I say,
thinking about
how on the bus he wouldn't
let me free from my seat.
Kept me trapped
by his legs.
I remember how the boys laughed
and the girls
hollered
and pointed.

I remember how
my Lizzie
whopped Jace a good one
right upside his head
with her notebook
till he set me free.

Then how Liz
grabbed my hand
and pulled me away.

I don't love
Jace Nelson, if that's what
you're asking,
I say.

Mari leans close.

But do you think
he's cute?

I shrug.

Why? Because if
I was going to pick

someone from school
it would be
Alex Cain.

I don't say
a word
but *he* is a hottie.

That's what I thought,
Mari says to
my silence.

She gives me an evil grin.

You like naughty boys,
don't you, Hope?
She says this with an old lady voice.

And I laugh right out loud.

35.

At home
now that the sun
is down,
I can see Liz's fear
myself.

In the bodies
of those kittens
grown cold.

Fear
smeared in the night sky
and
at the edges of our room

I worry
that maybe,
maybe
Liz will follow
those kittens

on outta here

and leave me
alone

for good.

36.

Lizzie,
I think,
are you okay?

When
are you coming back
home?

37.

Once,
me and Lizzie,
we fought

so loud
and so hard
that

Momma put us
in the front
yard
and said,
You two wild
things
fight it out
out here.

We did.

We fought,
hollering at
each
other
until
I took

a
swing at
Lizzie,
connecting
with her
chin.

That's it!
she said.
That is it!

She knocked me
to the
ground
and sat on my back.

Say uncle,
she said.

She pushed my
face into the
ground.
Into that sharp
Florida
grass.

Say uncle,
she said,
or eat dirt.

Never,
I said.
Never
ever.

I ate dirt and grass,
both.

But
I never said
uncle.

38.

Right before they
took Lizzie away.

We sat in the sun,
school still in
for a few weeks more.
Late spring everywhere,
flowers
poking up
here and there,
peach trees blooming like crazy.

Miss Pearl,
Lizzie said that day,
wants me to interview
someone
I have a lot of respect for.
For a report.

Oh yeah?
I said
all worried
about math
and how confused
I was even at

just-about end of the year.

That's right,
Liz said.
She pulled the ponytail holder
from her hair
that fell long around her shoulders.

The sun shone on her,
making her auburn hair
golden and
bright.

So?
I said.

So
I picked you,
Liz said.
You're the person
I respect most.

Me?
I was so surprised
even math

was forgotten.
For a second.

Sure,
I said, pleased.
Wow.
Okay.

Liz took her pencil,
licked the tip,
and said,

What's your name?

Oh, Lizzie,
I said,
my face going red
at the attention,
you already know that.

This
is an interview.
You have to
answer.
Your name?

It's Hope Kristine Chapman.

Smells of roses
blew past
us.

The sun was
hot and yellow-white.
I fanned my face
with homework.

What are your goals?

Goals? I said,
I didn't have a-one.
Not yet.
They came overnight,
much later.

Hmmmm,
I said.
What did I want
from me?
For me?

You have to have
one goal,
Liz said.
Me,
she tapped her chest,
I want
to sing.

Well, me too,
I said.
I want to be a famous
singer.
With you,
Liz.

Okay then,
she said.
And like she meant it
Liz wrote
the words down.

Hey.
Maybe you and me and Momma
could be famous
together,

I said.
The Chapman Girls,
Country and Western's Best Family
Trio.

Liz made an
ugly face at
that.
Just with you,
she said.

Is that your onliest goal?

For now,
I said.
That's it.

Lizzie closed her eyes
chewed on her pencil.
The sun
seemed to pat her
head.

My second goal,
she said,

her words all breathy,
is to get the hell outta here.

39.

Looking back,
I can see
Lizzie
meant what she
said.

Her going, I mean.
Her getting the hell
outta here.

Now
I think of my sister,
gone from our town
but still in
Florida.

I close my eyes
tight.

What is she sick of?
Is the hospital
far enough away for
her?

Or is death
really what she's after?

40.

Bad dreams.

More than a month ago.
The sky brittle.

Crying
all night it seems.

Then wake with a start.
Shaking.
Sweaty.

Lizzie?
I whispered my
sister's name.

But Momma
I know
came in here earlier.

She led my sleepy sister out.

Why?
I asked.

She's been sick,
Momma said to me.

When?
I said.

Right now, Hope,
Momma said.
Right now.

Momma?
I called out,
my voice slight with fear.

You go back to sleep in there,
Hope,
Momma said.
You stay in there.
I don't want you catching
what Liz has.

There were voices in my head.
The dream cried on,
sounding too real for comfort.

I got under my blanket and pillow
and prayed myself
back to sleep.

41.

Dreams.

Don't I
buy you clothes?

Don't I
get you pretty things?

Don't I
take good care of you?

You hush now.
Hush up.

Stop that
crying.

Shhh.
Shhh.
Quiet.

42.

I'm sitting on the front porch,
thinking how I miss Liz,
watching the torn screen
flap in the wind,
when Mari comes
riding down the driveway
on her bike.

Let's go, she says.
You and me. We're
headed to the river.

I see
Mari carries a picnic
basket and a plastic
bag full of stuff.
Her purple hair seems
to soak up
the sun.

For a moment, I
sit quiet
wondering if I should
go anywhere fun
with Lizzie waiting in a hospital.

Then Mari says,
You don't have a choice.
Get up, Hope. You
are coming with me,
like it or not.

Okay, I say,
'cause I am too
tired to argue
with her.

It's a long trip.
A hot trip.
Two miles away.
Down back roads.
Past an orange grove,
past a drug store
and a 7-Eleven.

Every once in a while
I can smell
the ocean
in the air
even though we are
headed in the

opposite direction.

But I know
when me and Mari get
there
that river will be so pretty,
with its white banks
and trees that scratch at the
water.

What's in the basket?
I ask her, pumping along.

It's a surprise,
Mari says, pedaling close,
balancing the big picnic basket
on the bar of her bike.

She never hunches
over the way
I would if her bike was
mine.
She drives in the
sitting-straight-up
position,

balancing.

Mom let me
pick out everything
from the store,
Mari says, looking at me.
She feels guilty 'cause
I had to babysit
Mattie all night
while she and Dad
were "out of town."

She makes her
fingers quotes.

Mattie is four years old
and stick skinny
except for a little
pot belly.

My momma never feels guilty,
I say to my best friend, telling
the truth.

This bike

I ride proves it.

Rickety
old thing
held together by bits
of paint and
leftover ribbons
that Liz and
I tied all over it.

The decorations are from
Before
when me and Lizzie
pretended we were in a
parade.

I start to say,
Can't be away
from
home
too long.

I start to say,
I promised Liz I'd be back
soon.

But Liz,
I remember,
is not there.

43.

Down
to the river me and
Mari
go, pedaling hard.

I try not to think.
(Lizzie!)
Try not to remember.
(All those baby kittens!)
Try to keep going.

The air is thick and hot,
storm-ready.

I watch as clouds
boil up
in the sky.
Things darken
in the east
where, if we headed that way,
we would run into the
ocean.

What's in the bag?
I say.

Mari grins at me.
Pads.

Pads?
What kinda pads?
For writing?

Has she
brought something
to help me
get started on my
writing career?

You know,
Mari says,
sanitary pads.
Sanitary *napkins*.
Kotex.
Tampons.
Mari is loud
—proud.
Twelve and three-quarters,
four months older than me,
and proud of *that*, too.

What?
My voice swoops into the air
and my foot almost
slips off the pedal,
You mean . . .

She nods.
Yep. I started,
she says.

She grins at me,
triumphant.
I am a woman now.

Her purple hair
waves in the wind
like a flag.

The Womanhood Flag.

I don't know
what you're grinning about,
I say,
and smile too.
I don't want that to ever happen.

I'm staying a girl all my life.
No blood for me,
thank you very much.

(I want to be
just a little girl
though truth be told
I don't have that.
Not now.)

And like that
I remember.

Momma so mad.

Another baby,
she said.
But not for long,
she said.
I'm getting
rid of this one,
she said.

Like I should have
you two.

Now big drops of rain
fall from the sky.

Mari glances up.
Cross your fingers
it doesn't rain too hard,
she says.
You know
I can't get water in my ears.

Mari has tubes.
Not sure why.
But she's not allowed to get
her ears wet.

If you ask me,
that's too bad,
seeing we live close to rivers
and the ocean
and, to top it all off,
she has a pool.

It *is* gonna rain,
I say.
Look at those clouds.

The words come outta
my mouth
and right then
the sky opens up
wide and dumps
buckets of water on us.

We pedal, heads down.

Now I carry the lunch
and her womanhood
bag.

Mari tries
to keep her ears covered,
but one hand won't
do for both sides of her head.

Cars plow through water,
splashing us.
Little rivers run on the street.

Rain streams down my face.
I am soaked clear through.

We move to the side of the road,
the whole world gray
like Florida becomes
in a good rain.

Mari pulls out a
sanitary napkin.

Put that away,
I say, looking
toward the road.
Somebody might see it.

You want me to go deaf?
she says.

She plucks the filling from a
couple of pads
and puts a wad in each ear.

I'm ready now, let's go.
Mari motions with her chin
and I can just see
cotton coming from her head
like her stuffing has come loose.

I laugh all the way to the river.
Not thinking about
Lizzie.
Not remembering
all those baby kittens.
And not one small thought
of the other baby
that might have been
a sister.

44.

This is last summer,
when Liz was happy.

Shh!
Liz whispered to me.
Stop that giggling.

Momma slept downstairs
after a long night.

All I see is your butt,
I said
and Liz laughed.

She turned around
and looked down from the attic
opening at me,
to where I waited below.

Shh,
she said again.
If Momma finds us
doing this there'll
be no secret clubhouse.

I used the shelf
to push myself through
the tiny crawl space and then,
turning around myself,
gazed at Liz.

She
covered her mouth
hiding a smile.

This,
she said
when she settled,
this is the Chapman Girls' Hideout.

The attic was fire-hot.
So hot it was hard to breathe.
And dusty, too.
Whew!

Liz looked serious all the sudden.

What will we do here?
I said.

A candle flame flickered.
I could only find a stub
with just a little light left in it.
Liz lit it
before I sat
next to her.

Ah,
said Liz,
like she was wise.
We come here for meetings.
We come here when
things are too tough in the real world.

I looked at her.

We meet here to regain our
composure.

Huh?
What's that mean?
I said.

That means,
she took a big breath

like she felt annoyed at having to
explain,
that means when things are tough,
this is the hideout.

My hands sweat
and my face sweat and
sweat rolled offa me
all over my body.
I thought sure there would be
a wet butt print on the floor
when I got up.

Say the solemn vow after me,
Liz said in a low voice.

Okay.
I answered in the same voice
she used.

When things get tough ...
When things get tough ...

When life is rough ...
When life is rough ...

The Chapman girls . . .
The Chapman girls . . .

Will take only enough.
Will take only enough.

She stopped like she was thinking of
more words
that rhymed with tough. I
tried to help
but my mind drew a blank,
because
I was gonna have heatstroke
maybe.

Our place to hide,
she said,
and sweat drops
splatted
on the wooden floor.

Now Liz wore a little dirt bead
necklace that wasn't
there when we first climbed into the
attic.

Our place to hide,
she said again
and licked her lips.

Our place to hide,
I said.
But I thought,
Next time we'll bring us something to
drink.

Is up here inside.
Is up here inside.

Where no one ...
Where no one ...

Not no one ...
Not no one ...

Will know our secrets.

I tilted my head and whispered,
That didn't rhyme.

Say it anyway,

she said.
I want our first Chapman Girls' Club
meeting
finished for the day.
It's too damn hot
in here.

I gasped.
You said *damn*.

Liz nodded, her
face pink in the
candlelight.
Say it, quick!

What was it you said?

Will know our secrets.
Oh yeah, will know our secrets.

She leaned over the candle
and blew it out.

Let's go swimming,
she said.

45.

One night
I hear crying
and it's not Lizzie
because she is at
the hospital.

My nightmares are back?
I think.

But when I walk
from my room
down the
hall
looking for
the dream,
I find
Momma.

Crying and drinking.

Her mascara has smudged
and her nose is red
and when she talks
her voice
is all run together

and plump
with words.

Oh, Hope,
she says,
I sure do
miss your
daddy.
I sure do.

46.

One Sunday afternoon, two weeks
after the gun, I
sit eating a peanut butter and
guava jelly sandwich
watching wrestling on
TV.

Trying not to think
of Lizzie
so far away in the hospital.
I did think, though.
I thought all about her.
I couldn't help it.
Even as the wrestlers
holler at each other,
pound on each other,
I think about
my sister.

Momma
waltzes in the living room
smiling
like nothing else matters.
Guess where we're headed?
she says.

She waves her hands,
flapping like she might fly
if she gets going
fast enough.

I don't look at her.
My favorite wrestler,
Big King,
is beating the tar outta
a little muscle-y guy called
Lightning Bolt.

Hope?

I grunt. Keep
watching.
Not not thinking.

You listening?
Momma's hand flapping
stops.

I nod, but I'm not.
Body slam
goes Lightning Bolt

onto the tarp.
His face twists in pain.

Big King throws himself
over Lightning Bolt.
Then,
Psycho Killer Man appears
outta nowhere.
Leaping over the ropes
to save
Lightning Bolt.

Momma
stands in front of the TV
and switches it off with her behind.

Guess where we are
off to right this very minute,
she says again.

Hey now,
I say.
I was watching that.

I have a sadness in my mouth

that never seems to leave.

You got to know,
Momma says,
I don't give a white rat's ass
what you were watching.
She's not happy now.
I am trying to talk to
you,
she says,
and I mean business.
You listening good?
We're leaving.

Where to?
I say.

I make my eyes big.
I look at Momma
like I care about
what she will say.

To visit
my Lizzie
girl,

she says.
Momma comes closer,
leans on my chair,
putting a hand on
either side of
my knees.
And you can see her too,
she says.
Her smile is back.

The four times before
when Momma visited
my sister
I sat
in the waiting room
while she whispered
to her behind closed
doors.

Really?
I say, not caring for TV
anymore.
Hoping to move the
sadness away.
My heart thumps.

Swear it's true?

I do swear it,
Momma says with a laugh.
Go do your hair
and change your shirt.
Don't want us looking
like white trash.

She adjusts her bra strap
with a finger
then
sucks something
outta her teeth.

Hurry it up,
she says.

I'm going,
I say.
My knees have gone weak
(I'm so excited to see Lizzie).
I run to the bedroom.
My whole self goes pink
thinking of the visit.

Wuh-hoo!
I pump a fist
in the air.

Keep it down,
Momma hollers in to me.

She turns on the radio.
Elton John sings.
Momma joins in.

Her voice is
prettier than
summer rain.
It is light and
warm.

And we are going
to see Lizzie.

47.

I want
to tell her all
about Ian St. Clair.

I want to hug her up
close.

I want to say,
Let's you and me
get outta
here.

But Liz
is blurry-eyed.
And she won't say
a thing.

Still,
when Momma
leaves the room for a smoke,
my sister
reaches for
my hand,
her fingers weak.

Be careful,
she says.

The words come out
sounding fat
like Liz's tongue is a sponge
filled with water.

I lean close.
What's that?
I say.

My eyes fill with tears,
but none spill over.
It has been so long
since I have cried,
my eyes feel like
hot, dry
cement.

Shhh,
Liz says,
shhh.

She gives my hand

a small squeeze,
light,
like she has no
strength.

I clutch her fingers
touch her hair
feel confused
at **be careful**.

I say,
All right.
I will.

There's a window
in this room,
small and square.
It's filled with mesh screen
to keep people out.

(To keep people in?)

Late afternoon sun
touches the carpet.
That blue-green spot is

brighter
than the rest.
Warm-looking.

The air conditioner
turns on
with a low hum.
The curtains give a gentle wave,
like they say
good-bye.

And all the time I watch,
I think,
Be careful.
Be careful.
And I wonder,
of what?
Be careful of what?

Do I tell Momma?
I say to Liz.
Do I let her know
to be careful too?

I talk close to my sister's face

in a soft voice.

Her breath smells funny.
Do I smell like peanut butter?
Guava jelly?

Liz tries to turn
her head
but she can't.
It's like
it weighs too much.

But she makes a face.
Her teeth just showing.
A thin and almost-not-there
face.

Momma comes bouncing in then,
her voice announcing herself,
too loud for this
quiet moment.

You getting her to talk,
Hope?
Momma says.

I couldn't get her to say
nothing.
Doctor says it's normal.

Momma waits
to hear from me,
something she doesn't do.

She talking to you?

Liz's eyes are closed now.
She's moved her hand
from mine.
Like we weren't
touching
at
all
before.

I don't know why
but I lie.

She didn't say a thing,
I say.
I just been whispering to her.

Talking
about Ian St. Clair.

I don't look Momma in the eye.
Instead,
I pat Liz's long auburn hair.
Braided.

Let me say one
last thing to your sister
here,
Momma says.
You go wait by the front desk.

So I go . . .
sort of.

Really I stand right next
to the door
of my sister's room.
But I can't hear anything
being
said, even though I strain to.

48.

Momma got me a
Ouija board last
Christmas.

I am sure it's broken.

Doesn't work, not even a little bit.
Unless
I help it out some.

Except . . .

Before,
just after her crying started,
me and Liz
played on that ol' board
sitting on the living room floor,
game propped
on our knees.

I made up answers to
her questions.

Does Matthew Earl
like me better'n a friend?
she said.

Yes,
the board answered,
with me just
smiling.

Am I pretty?

Beautiful,
the board said,
me wanting to laugh.

Will I die young?

Will
I
Die
Young

49.

I turned to ice,
dripping slow,
leaking,
in the heat of that question.

Will I die
young?

What kind of
question was that?
I swallowed,
glanced at my sister.

She stared at the planchette,
waiting for an answer.

Behind her
I saw the night sky
held back
by the single French door
and that yellowed lace curtain.

I saw the pale line
of the part on her head,

her hair, wavy,
and falling forward.

I have always wanted hair that color.
Not so blond as mine is.

It's not saying anything,
Liz said.

Give it time.
I said in a whisper.

How do I fix
this?
I thought.
I have to take care of
Lizzie.
And she has to take care of me.

There was something
heavy
in my stomach.

But I jiggled

the beige pointer
like it was getting a breath of
life.

It's going,
Liz said.

She straightened,
waiting.
The board on our knees.
Our fingertips just
touching
the tear-shaped playing piece.

I glanced again at Liz.
Couldn't see the freckles on her face,
just that crooked part of hers
in her hair.

Would it be a lie this time too?
I wondered.
You will live a long, peaceful life,
I wanted to say.

But before I could do anything,
the pointer started
on its own.

In a smooth,
slow,
steady
pace
it made its way down
to the word
good-bye.

And stopped.
Just stopped.

Liz looked at me
and I know my
eyes were surprised.

You moved that,
I said.

I didn't,
she said.

You did,
I said.

She shook her head
no.

I spoke too
fast.
You're staying
with me forever,
I said,
knocking the board
from our knees,
hugging her
close.

She didn't hug me
back.

I mean that,
I said.

I mean it.

But that awful feeling,
that I-can't-breathe feeling,
would not go
away.

50.

Here's the deal:

On the drive home
from the hospital
and my first visit
with her

I think of Liz's words,
to be careful.
I think about them
the whole hour
home.

And I cannot figure it out.

Why be careful?
Of what?
Of who?

Does something wait in the dark
for me?

Did something wait in
the dark for Liz?

I think hard about
her changes.
Think of when
the crying began.
When was it my sister
decided going was
better than
staying?
When was it I
had to be
careful?

51.

Why,
Liz said to me,
when I came home
one morning
from a sleepover.

Why have you been
gone so long?

What?
I said
and threw
my backpack on my
bed, turning to
Liz.

Why?

Liz was angry,
really angry.

I was at Mari's,
I said.
It was a sleepover.

Her face went red and I saw
tears come into her
eyes.

She walked up close to me.
So close I could
see where her bottom teeth
overlapped
just a bit.

Her voice was a fat whisper.
You,
she said, pointing
right in my face,
you
are
always
gone.

For the rest of the day,
no matter how hard
I tried to get her to,
Lizzie
wouldn't speak to me.

That night,
when the sun
tucked itself in
Lizzie
started to whimper
then
cry.

Shut up!
Momma hollered.
Shut up
shut up
shut up!

Momma slammed the door
between our room
and hers. I
heard the lock
click.

Lizzie's voice
grew
weary
and I moved from my

bed
to where she lay
curled in a lump.

Let me under
the covers
with you,
I said.
Let me.
Her crying scared me.
Scared me
something awful.

I'm sorry,
Liz
said in her
weeping,
I'm sorry. I'm sorry
to be mean to
you, Hope.

You're not mean,
Liz,
I said.

You should stay gone,
she said.
You should stay gone
long as you can.

I climbed into
bed with
my sister
tickled her back
and her arms
and her face
trying to calm her
sobs.

52.

Hey, Hope?
It's Mari on the phone.
Wanna come over,
go swimming?

It's the day after the picnic
and nothing
got me last night
when I crawled into bed
and slid beneath the covers.

You know it,
I say.

I change into my suit.
It's getting small on me.
Growing bosoms,
at last.

Momma says
becoming a woman
is taking longer for
me than Lizzie.
Man, is she
right.

Lizzie
looks way older,
more than a year older
than me.
She's bigger breasted,
smaller waisted,
more grown-up.

Now I slip shorts
over my bathing suit
and go into the
room I shared with
Liz.

It's so lonely here
without her.

I walk
into my room
only to go to sleep.
At night it's harder to
see the empty bed
but easier to sleep
without
the crying.

Before,
not even that long ago,
I got ready
to go somewhere
with Mari.

Liz watched me,
then said,
Where you going?
Where you going, Hope?

To Mari's,
I said.

Stay this time,
she said.
Stay with me.

What? Uh-uh.
Go visit a friend of your own,
I told her,
brushing my hair.
Go hang out with
Amanda or Cheri.

Not hanging out with
them anymore.
Liz looked away
like she was embarrassed.

You fighting?

Nope,
she said.
And kept looking away
out the window away
away from my eyes away.

We're still
friends.
I'm just not
doing so much
with anyone
anymore.

A deep breath.

Besides, Momma doesn't
want me to go so much.
She wants me here,

Liz said.
Not off.

When'd she start
to care if you're here?
I said.

Lizzie let out
a sigh
big as our room.
I guess it's me, too.
I don't feel like going.

Don't feel like going?
I said.
That's weird, girl.

You go on,
Liz said
after a moment.
You go, Hope.
I'll stay.

So I left.
Went off with Mari.

Left
Liz at home, watching me
leave.

Sometimes
I would go
for a whole weekend.

Liz, she would
stare after me,
follow
out onto the porch,
and
watch me pull
my bike
from the falling-down
garage.
She
would watch me pedal
down the street
away from
her.
Waving good-bye
like she didn't quite mean it
like she needed Amanda

or Cheri
like I needed Mari.

I'd look back
and there
she'd be
just a dot on the porch,
still standing
there.

Alone.

This memory
is like bricks on me now.
Heavy as a wall.
My sister standing there

alone.

53.

Some days
I miss Liz
so that it feels like
a hand is tight around
my throat.

It feels like
she has been gone years
not just two and a half
weeks.

I remind myself
what Momma has said—
that we can visit Liz
anytime we want
now.

I remind myself
how we could
go every day,
if we wanted.

But.

I have my business,

Momma says,
when I ask for us to go
more often.

54.

At Mari's house we:

1. Swim in her pool

2. Picnic on the deck

3. Talk about boys from school.

But all the while
I remember my sister,
before,
standing on the porch
watching me
go.

55.

On the way out
of town,
stuck back in the woods
with only a hand-painted
sign to mark it,
is Miss Freeman's store.

Momma calls Miss Freeman
white trash,
with a capital **W**
and a capital **T**. Even
though she made us all
that food
when Daddy left us
for good.
Even though
me and Liz stayed
with Miss Freeman
whilst Momma
had her guests.
Even though
we've lived near her
for years now.

Miss Freeman is fat

and old and
missing teeth.

WT,
Momma says.

Three teeth gone,
all right there in the
front, to be exact.

She can't read or write,
neither.

WT,
Momma says.

I've seen Miss Freeman in her store
with
blacks and whites,
men and women,
babies and teenagers.
She treats everyone the same.
Real nice.

She runs this used clothing
place just off the river.
Four old rooms
built from cinder block
with handmade
wooden tables
piled high with clothes
of every kind.

I've found me some
pretty stuff in there,
sometimes as cheap as
twenty-five cents an outfit.

On Thursday afternoon,
on the way to see Lizzie,
Momma and me
stop to shop.

Momma doesn't buy from used
clothing stores,
not for herself.
But she wanted something
for Liz.

And I could do
with a pair of cutoffs
myself.

The store is crowded
because of a
buy-one-get-one-free
sale.
Two for twenty-five cents
today
only,
says a hand-lettered sign
out on the road,
with an arrow pointing this way
to the store.

I wonder,
Who wrote that
sign for Miss Freeman?
One of her grown boys?
A neighbor?

I would have done it
for her
had I known.

Can't beat two for twenty-five cents
with a stick,
Momma says.

She finds a little
nightshirt with a puppy
on the front
for my sister.

I want her out of
those hospital clothes,
she says,
talking to herself.

I'm lucky and find shorts
almost the second we walk in.
A pocket is missing,
but what do you expect
for twelve and a half pennies?

Momma and I
get in line behind
a man whose arms
are filled to overflowing
with clothing.

When he reaches the counter
he pulls out his wallet,
thick with money.

Miss Freeman sees us behind
him.
Ms. Chapman,
she says with a nod.
Hope.
I nod back.

Then,
How you doin', mister?

Terrific,
he says,
and smiles a full-toothed grin.

I'm sure he
bleaches his teeth

they are so white.

Or maybe he's a dentist.

But
what would a dentist
be doing in here with a
big ol' stack of used clothes?

Let's count this up,
Miss Freeman says,
gathering things by twos.

Twenty-five, fifty, seventy-five, a dollar.
Twenty-five, fifty, seventy-five, two
dollars,
she says.

Momma eyes the man.

I know why, straight up.
All that money.

Miss Freeman keeps counting.
Twenty-five, fifty, seventy-five, four
dollars.
Twenty-five, fifty, ...
Soon she's up to eight dollars.

Momma leans close to the man.
You have a big ol' family,
don't you?
she says.

I work with orphans,
he says,
shifting till he faces
Momma.

And you are?
he says to her.

Orphans?
Miss Freeman says.
She smiles.
Let me throw in a few things free.

She piles clothes
onto the man's stuff.

You good man,
Momma says,
never giving her name.
That only comes

with repeat business.

I look away.
I can see what
Momma's doing and it worries me.
We're supposed to see
Lizzie today.

Sometimes,
when this happens,
when she meets someone,
I end up sitting in the car
for hours
waiting for Momma
and whoever
to come out of
whatever room they've
chosen.

Still,
we're close enough to home.
I've seen Miss Freeman walking
to work.
I can walk it too.

But what about Lizzie?

Ten dollars and seventy-five cents,
Miss Freeman says.
And I didn't count some of it.
Will you tell the children
it's a gift from me?

Orphan man nods,
hands her a twenty.

Yes, ma'am,
I surely will.

Miss Freeman grins.

Momma moves in close to
the man.

Let's see,
Miss Freeman says,
and she starts counting
out change for him.

Add their things too,

orphan man says,
and puts the nightshirt
and my shorts on top
of his pile.

I'll take care of this,
he says to Momma.

Now there,
Momma says,
touching him with her
fingertips.
You don't need to do that,
she says.

The added twenty-five cents
throws Miss Freeman.

She blinks
a couple of times
and I know right then
and there
that not only can she not
read
and

write,
math isn't her strong point either.

Miss Freeman,
I say,
just add . . .

Hush now,
Momma says,
giving me a stinging
pinch on the arm.

The man smiles pretty
at Momma and
she smiles pretty at him.
All those white
teeth.

I feel my ears go hot.

A mile and half from home,
I think.
I can walk that easy.
Oh, Lizzie.

Miss Freeman
gives the man some change,
two fives,
and three ones.

You owe me
more than this,
he says,
his voice loud.

More?
Miss Freeman says.

I notice her hands shake.
I feel sad and
small inside.
I feel old.
And dirty.

I try to stare
a bullet into that cheating
orphan man's heart.

He nods and sneaks
the loose change

and bills into his pocket
while holding out his other hand.

Miss Freeman gives him
a ten-dollar bill that's
wrinkled
and old looking.

And a quarter, too,
he says.

Of course,
Miss Freeman says.

She rings NO SALE
and the cash register dings open.
I look away
when she gives him the money.

We all walk
out of the store,
though my feet
are stone,
into the bright Florida
sunlight, and Momma

lets out a giggle.

I get into our
car, while Momma whispers
to orphan man.

I think,
I cannot stand his guts.
I cannot stand him at all.
I like Miss Freeman.

Follow me,
Momma says to him.
She gets into
our car, slamming
the door
shut.

And he follows us in
his fancy blue car.

What about Lizzie, Momma?
I say.
We're supposed to see
her today.

But Momma ignores me.

Just
down the road,
orphan man signals
Momma with his car lights.

He turns off next to
the Winn-Dixie
and Momma pulls up behind.

What's he planning?
Momma asks no one.
But she has
this laugh on her face.

Orphan man
gathers up all the clothes
and throws them
into a Dumpster.

Hey,
I say.
Hey.

Momma laughs her head off.
Slaps at the steering wheel.

Boy,
Momma says,
he made some money
on that one.

On Miss Freeman,
I think,
but I say,
What about our clothes?
My shorts?

Quit being so damn selfish,
Momma says.
She slaps my leg,
leaving a pink handprint
right above my knee.

Just leave me here,
I say,
staring out the window,
away from her.
And Momma does.

When I can't see
their cars anymore,
when they are gone
from my sight,
I peer into the Dumpster.

The clothes are way
at the bottom, in something
that looks like
melted chocolate ice cream
and wilted lettuce. I can't
see my shorts
or Lizzie's nightshirt
only the stuff orphan man
stole.

I start walking
and head to Mari's,
hoping she's home,
and that whole long walk
I keep hearing
Miss Freeman say,
Will you tell the children
it's a gift from me?

And orphan man,
him saying,
Yes, ma'am, I surely will.

And I hope
I hope
Lizzie didn't
plan on us coming.

56.

When did Momma
get like this?

Cheating an old woman,
a neighbor who's helped us,
and then laughing about it?

I don't remember
when that
happened.

And I usually
remember
everything.

57.

The next time
Momma and me
see Liz
she's up,
tied in a sitting/leaning position
in a wheelchair.

Why is she tied?
I ask, but no one
answers me.

Momma's
spent some time
whispering at Liz,
right in her ear.
Liz's head never moves.
She never says
a thing to our
momma
who gets angry
and stays that way
the whole visit.

When
it's my turn

with my sister, I hurry
to her side.

Lookit what I can do, Liz,
I say.

I push her to the stereo.
Momma's gone,
I say.
Went to take a smoke.

Liz opens her eyes
slow.
Her head doesn't move
at all.

I put on the CD
Singing to You,
her favorite Ian St. Clair
song,
and before the music begins
I say,
Me and Mari have been practicing.

Then I roll a magazine tight

to use as a microphone,
look around to make sure
no one's watching,
and sing with Ian,
because she likes him,
and I like him,
and so does Mari.
I step here and there
on the blue-green carpet,
swing my hips,
slap my hands in time
with Ian's voice,
in front of chairs
empty of people.

Liz watches from half-open eyes.

When I'm done,
three nurses
step from the doorway
and clap.

My face burns.

Real good, one says.

I bob my head
thank you
and want to melt away.

I kneel at Lizzie's feet.
I'm thinking about
dancing at the talent show,
I say,
once school starts.
What do you think?

You'd win,
Liz says.
Her voice almost not
there.

I hug her up close.
Love mixed
with pain
rises in my
chest.

I sure do miss you,
I say.
I sure wish you'd

come home.
So does
Momma.

Liz's body goes tight.
She says,
Never,
so no one
but me can hear.

She says,
I'll never go back
home.

What's going on?

Momma's voice startles
me, makes me
jump, but not Liz
who still
doesn't move.

You talking, baby?
Momma leans so close
I can smell cigarettes

on her breath.

Liz
lets her head hang.

She's not speaking,
I say.
I can't keep the
lie-sound outta
my voice.

So I see,
Momma says.
Her eyes squinch
into a line.

All that ride
home I hear
in my
head, Never.
Never.
Never.
I'll never go back
home.

So where will
Liz go?

And what will I do
when she gets there?

58.

We get home
late that night.
Momma swings into
Burger King for me,
then
stops at Sizzler
and gets herself
a thick steak,
baked potato,
and steamed broccoli.

Part of my pay,
Momma says
when she runs the
carry-out boxes
to the car
and I wonder who
she knows here
at the Sizzler.

We drive home quick.
Hurry dinner in
so it stays nice
and hot.
I pull out two plates

to set the table.
We sit down to eat.

Outside
the evening sky
is filled with
pink clouds
lined with purple and
gold.

Bats swoop chasing
mosquitoes.

It seems the
air trembles with
color while the sun
goes down.

I watch
an early evening dragonfly
swish through
the air.

A country band sings in
the background

and at the table
I sing harmony with
Momma.

Momma has herself one big
range.
She can sing tenor to high soprano
and never miss a note.

There we are
just us two,
singing eating enjoying
each other's company,
when the phone rings
and

I almost
don't answer.

I love singing with Momma,
love the colors
in the sky,
love this hamburger.

Go get that,
Momma says,
cutting into her
potato.

At the last
moment
I run to grab
the phone.

A man asks for Momma by name.

Another customer,
I whisper to her,
gesturing.

Momma jumps to her feet
her face going
funny.

What?
she shouts.

Then she runs

hard
pushing me away,
not quite knocking me
to the ground.

What?
she shouts again,
then puts the phone to
her ear
to listen.

What do you mean?
she says,
and I can see
that steak sitting
in her mouth.

My heart pounds
so hard I feel it in
my face.

The french fries
smell like
grease.

My hands sweat.
I glance
away
away.

Outside
the dragonfly
swings
through
the air.
And there goes
a bat.

My eyeballs strain
at my head,
like they want to get
free,
like they have
seen something
I cannot understand.

Was it an accident?
Momma says,
then she yells so

that I have to
cover my ears.
And
I
yell
too.

I'm coming,
she says.

She
doesn't even hang up
the phone, just drops it
like it's too hot to hold.
It hits the ground with a
pop!

What is it?
I say
and my voice
is loud too.

Stay with Mari,
Momma says,

running toward the door,
grabbing the car keys
as she goes.

Why?
I say.

It's Liz,
Momma says,
from the front door.

Out behind my mother
the sky has lost all the pink.
It's gone a green sea
color, readying for dark.

She tried it again,
Momma says.

Momma's out the door
into the evening
and I follow

looking for that

dragon-
fly
but
it
is
g
o
n
e
.

59.

Again?
Again?

60.

For a moment
I am sure that I will
die
too,
standing there holding that
Whopper
waiting on Momma to say
something,
anything.

I cannot breathe.
Not at all.
Not one bit of
air
goes into my lungs.

She alive?
I say,
using up the last
of the oxygen
there was in me.

For now,
Momma says.
She slams

the car door
shut.

Then I watch her
drive
away,
wondering how she knew
what that call
would be.

61.

Can I spend the night?
I say to Mari
when she opens the
front door
to my tapping.

We have the house to
ourselves,
Mari says,

Mom and Dad
are at the greenhouses
checking the watering
system.
They'll be late.

My hands still shake
because of Liz.

I rode my bike fast
to get here
letting the hot air blow
in my eyes,
drying

tears before they could
appear.

Cool,
I say
and breathe deep
the Mari scent.

Just you and me?

Well almost,
Mari says.
Mattie's here.

Mattie
makes me crazy.

She's a
spitter.

Every time she sees me,
she lets go
a glob of spit,
sailing it through the air,
aimed right at me.

Now I roll my eyes at Mari.

Mattie's sleeping, though,
Mari says.
As long as we're quiet . . .

We turn on Ian St. Clair
music
and sing.

I do the harmony.
Mari is the melody.

The first song ends.
I throw my arms out
for the grand finale,
wishing my sister
could see me singing this
with background
music,
when all the sudden I hear
ka-too-ee.

A gob of spit

comes at me.
I jump.
Mattie's goober
hits right where I was.

She's awake,
Mari says.

I see,
I say.

And I wish
it was Liz
standing there.
Even if she was
spitting,
and trying
to make me
mad,
though she wouldn't,
not at fourteen,

I wish Mattie was Liz.

62.

That night,
as darkness fills Mari's bedroom
and presses on my eyelids
like a pair of cold thumbs,
I remember Lizzie
telling me
why me and Lizzie
are best friends.

Here's the story,
Hope,
Lizzie said in my memory.
It was a warm day,
that telling,
full of sun
and cabbage moths
and summer smells.

Maybe I was four
when this happened,
she said.
So you were almost
three,
a little ol' thing,
with blond hair

so curly
Momma couldn't get a brush through it
when she tried.

Late one night,
when Daddy was working,
or that's the
way my memory
has it written,
Momma hollered
me awake.

And you, Hope,
just a baby, you cried.

Lizzie was quiet a moment
remembering.
Whimpers,
she said.
that's what your cries were.

So what happened?
How did we get to
be best friends?

For the telling,
we sat in the grass
at a park,
kids calling
back and forth to
each other
while they played
on the swings
and teeter-totter.

So I went to
Momma's room,
Liz said.

Her diaper's wet,
Momma said,
and her bottle's empty
again.

Lizzie sounded just like Momma
when she spoke
even wagging her head
the way Momma
does.

You took care of me,
I said, smiling at the thought,
didn't you, Lizzie?

She nodded.

So Momma handed the bottle to me.
Fill this,
she said.

Lizzie lowered
her voice
like maybe Momma listened in
though she was with a customer
and didn't even
know me and Lizzie were
at the park.

I saw you, Hope,
laying on your side
reaching for Momma.
She kept you pushed away
with one
hand.

Pushed away?
I said.

I
made my way into
the kitchen
turning on lights as I went,
Lizzie said.

No need in running into monsters in
the dark.
I pulled out a jug
of Kool-Aid,
and
poured that into your bottle.
No milk.
Momma needed it on her breakfast
cereal.

Right,
I said.

Then I ran,
noises chasing me,
back to Momma's room.

I gave the bottle to you, Hope,
but you just kept crying,
even after the nipple
was in your mouth.

Change her
and get her outta here,
Momma said.

I nodded, believing.
But Lizzie didn't stop the story.
I can't make the tape
stick right,
I told Momma.

And Momma screeched.
Now Lizzie
kept her voice,
her own,
when she used Momma's
words.
I said
change her and
get her outta here.

Come on, baby,
I said to you
and
Hope,
you reached for me
and
I pulled you from the bed.

That night
I put some of
my underwear
up and over
the diaper
to hold it on.

Me and Lizzie
we sat quiet
and listened
to the sounds of
kids playing.

Then I put my
arms around you and
held you close

so you wouldn't be
afraid.

I lay back
squinting at the sky
let the grass
poke at my skin
thought about Momma
pushing me away
like that.

That's when you and me,
Lizzie said,
that's when you and me
started sharing a room
and when we became
best friends.

63.

At night,
now that Liz is gone,
I am plagued with sad Liz memories.

In our room,
I climb into her bed.
I hope for no bad dreams.

I listen to the radio
tucked under my pillow
so Momma cannot
hear the sound.

Even this reminds me
of my sister. And
in the dark,
with Momma alone
or gone
or sometimes with a friend,
it is hard for me
to escape memories.

I am going crazy,
I say,
lying in bed.

I can almost feel Liz close by.
Almost hear her breathing.

Liz,
I say,
quit haunting me.

With the words out
I realize just how dead
that sentence sounds.

64.

One afternoon
Momma comes home from
a night and morning
away
(Miss Freeman
checked on me three different
times to make
sure I was okay
alone).

Momma's singing
a song from
Jesus Christ Superstar.

It's the song
Judas sings to Jesus
at the beginning of the album.

We've had the CD
forever
and Liz and I know all the words.

(Once Miss Freeman said,
I can hear you-all
singing your little

hearts out over there.
It's beautiful
just
beautiful the way
you-all blend.
And we said,
Thanks, Miss Freeman.)

We've sung parts
with Momma
and when she left us alone
for a day or two,
Lizzie and me
would play that music
over and over
at night
so we wouldn't be so afraid.

But with Lizzie away
I have to play our
music alone
and that makes the songs
lonely.

Momma's voice,

so throaty and low
makes me
remember being with
my sister.
Winter.
So cold
that the fireplace heat
did nothing in this room.
I could see our breath
when Liz and me whispered
together.

We were close,
like the petals of an
unopened rose.

Out of the blue
Liz said,
I don't like that
Floyd Brackney
at all.

Floyd Brackney
is one of Momma's
regulars.

Sometimes he comes here to pick
Momma up.

Lizzie's breath was warm
in my hair.
She had wrapped her arms
tight around my middle
and her chin dug into my shoulder
blade.

Me either,
I said.
Especially when he gets
that white spitty stuff
at the edges of his mouth.

He's like that
everywhere,
Liz said.
Yucky all over.
And his belly jiggles.

Right after she said *jiggles*,
I laughed and she said,
It's not funny, Hope.

But Lizzie laughed too.

Then she climbed from our
warm cocoon of a bed
and switched on the CD player.

Jesus Christ Superstar
came on, all those electric
guitars and electric organs.
Let's sing parts,
Liz said.

So we did.
I sang Judas and Liz sang Jesus
and our breath
puffed out like clouds
in the air
that cold night.

65.

Hope,
Momma says, the next
Saturday morning,
we got to go see Lizzie
today.
I hafta talk to a psychiatrist.

Momma looks at me side-eyed.

Damn,
she says,
this is costing me a helluva lotta money.
Good thing we got us a little savings.

I look
through my Ian St. Clair pictures.
Mari and me,
we're thinking of making
scrapbooks.
I've got enough stuff
to fill three volumes,
I bet.

Did you hear me?
Momma says.

We got to go see Lizzie.

All right,
I say.

It'll take the day,
Momma says.

She scratches
at her belly
near her piercing.
Since Momma plays the
guitar she never lets
her nails get too long.

I see she's
ready for the hospital.
Her shirt and skirt,
short and shiny,
makes her look uncomfortable.

Momma is blue jeans and halters
girl.
That's what she says.

And nice clothes when she's going out
at night.

I miss Liz,
I say.

And I do.
Something like hunger gnaws
at me when I
think of her
alone
at the hospital.

I have some things to give her,
I tell Momma
but she's busy
checking her hair in
the mirror.

Maybe my favorite Ian
picture,
I think.
Maybe a stuffed
animal so she

isn't all by
herself.

Pack us lunch,
Momma says.
We can't eat out every
time we travel to the hospital.
Get a couple of tangerines
out of the fridge.
And I want two sandwiches.

Yes, ma'am,
I say.

I fry
up bacon for
BLTs.

I get to see Lizzie.

66.

The first crush
I ever had on someone,
was a boy two years older
than me.

I was in fourth grade
and Adam Stevens
was in the fifth,
in class with Lizzie.
He sat right next to her.

(Lizzie had a crush
on Eric Bennion
even though he had some
fake teeth.)

Sometimes
I helped out in the
lunchroom, lining up cartons of
milk on red trays,
then trading slips of
paper with the teacher's
name written on them
for the drink.

And sometimes
Adam came through the line
to get his milk
(chocolate—two cartons).

One night
I told Lizzie,
I think I love him.
I think I love Adam Stevens.

Oh,
she said,
he likes you, too.

He does?
I said.

Yep,
Liz said.
He told me so at recess.

Why?
I said.
He just thinks you're pretty,
Lizzie said.

The cutest fourth grader
around.

Me and Liz sat in our room,
that long ago night,
drawing pictures for a
cartoon book we were making.

He told you that?
I asked.

Sure,
Liz said and gazed in my eyes.
You are the best little sister.
And nice.
Why wouldn't he like you?

For days
me and Lizzie talked
about Adam Stevens
until he came to school
with a big scab
on his chin.

After that,

my admirations turned to
Dennis and Desmond,
the twins in the fourth-grade
class right next door to
my room.

Later, of course,
I loved
Ian St. Clair. And so
did Lizzie, at least
a little.

He would love you,
Lizzie said not that long
before the gun.

That Ian
would love you if he
got the chance to know you,
she said.

You're the best little
sister anyone could have.
I love you, Hope. Why wouldn't
Ian?

And the way my sister
Lizzie talked,
anyone would believe her.

Maybe even Ian St. Clair.

67.

At the hospital
that afternoon,
Momma puts herself in Lizzie's room
right away,
pushing the door almost closed behind.
She's just out of
lockdown again.

You keep watch
while I talk to my baby,
Momma says.
There isn't even
a fake smile
on her face.

I don't.

Instead
I put my ear to the
crack of the door.

What is it that Momma
says to my sister
every time we come?

Why won't Lizzie talk to her?

Baby?
I hear Momma say.
Her voice is light as a balloon
filled with helium.
I hear the bed give a sigh,
like Momma sat down on the edge.

Baby,
she says,
what you been telling them doctors?
Now one of 'em wants to see me.

There's no answer.

Honey, Liz,
Momma says,
what you been telling them?

She waits.

You know there's them
secrets you and me have,
Momma says.

239

Them secrets no one
should know about.
You hear me, Liz? I
wish you'd open your
eyes, baby. You keep
them secrets to yourself, hear.
Do you hear me?

Has my heart stopped beating?
Am I alive here at the door?
Can I swallow?
Can I blink?
Or breathe
again?

Momma's voice
gets an edge to it.
My skin prickles.

You keep them secrets
quiet or worse is gonna happen.
To you first,
then to me. I'll
make sure about you getting it.
There's Hope still

at home.
You remember that,
right?

Now my heart beats
so I can see it
shaking my T-shirt.
Me? What about me?

Momma keeps talking.
The doctor
made mention of a diary.
Something you're writing in.
Where's that diary you got hid?
Is it that little pink book
you got for
Christmas last year?

I am like soup.
Can't stand.
My nose has quit working.
I gasp in
air through my mouth.

I hear a smack sound,

and then Momma
coming to the door.

I hop away fast,
and stand like I've been a guard
the whole conversation,
arms crossed and everything.

But I shake deep in my shoes,
and them just an old pair of Keds.

Your turn,
Momma says.
You try to make some sense of her.
I gotta smoke me a cigarette.

I watch Momma walk,
swinging her slim hips,
the whole way out before
I go in to Liz.
I shut the door tight behind me,
making sure I hear the click.

She's gone,
I say.

She's gone to smoke.

I kneel on the floor
near my sister.

Sweet Lizzie,
I say.
I whisper in hair,
Don't you worry
none about me.

I pet her face
and my tears
tears burn hot like a Florida sun.

She never opens her eyes,
but I know
Liz knows
I
am
here.

68.

We haven't been home
even
five minutes
when Momma
starts to work.
She tears our room up good
looking for that diary.

I help her go through
our bedroom things.
My mouth is
dry, watching.
Will Momma find it?
Will she?

Momma throws Liz's stuff
this way and that.
Help me look **now**, girl,
Momma says.

And I do, though
I don't want to, I pull books
outta the bookcase and
stuff from Liz's little
nightstand.

It's gotta be here somewhere,
Momma says once
and I can see she's madder
than a snake.

When she's tired from searching
she looks at me
and says, loud,
Get this mess cleaned up.

And I do as fast as I can.

69.

That night
after I've put all
the stuff back and my room
(our room, mine and Lizzie's)
is all cleaned,
Momma paces the house
looking everywhere.
There's a knock at the door.

Check who's there,
Momma says. And then a first,
I ain't seeing no one tonight.

It's Miss Freeman
standing in the light
of the front porch bulb.

Momma moves up beside me.
What?
she says,
not even hiding this time
that she doesn't
like Miss Freeman.

Miss Freeman doesn't

take a breath. Just speaks.
I don't know what's been going on,
she says.
Her voice is thin, coming through the
screen
like a moth batting
to get in.
But there's something,
Ms. Chapman.
I'm worried about
your girls.

What do you mean,
Miss Freeman?
Momma says,
and her voice
is like acid.

Something's going
on in there,
Miss Freeman says.
I don't know what,
but I know it's bad.
She taps at her
chest, big as a map.

I know it here,
she says.
And I've seen things.

Momma is real quiet.
So am I.
Outside, the night
is quiet too.
It's like everything listens,
waits
to hear what Momma will
say.

You need help, Ms. Chapman,
Miss Freeman says,
and I gasp.

But Momma's eyes narrow.
She stays quiet.

Then when she speaks, her
voice is low
as Miss Freeman's was.

You don't know nothing,

you fat bitch.
Momma closes the door
with a click.

Miss Freeman says louder,
There's something, Ms. Chapman,
I know it.
I know it in my heart.

Momma leans on the door.
She looks at me then says,
So that's what's under
all that fat. A heart.
She stands there,
leaning against the door
a long time,
lets out a shaky laugh.
Then she says,
Get to bed.

And I go, thinking,
Too many changes
going on here.
Thinking,
My momma is scared.

70.

Next morning
is Sunday.

Momma watches Miss Freeman
move off down
the road,
her dress fluttering
around her big
white calves.

When she's out of sight
Momma says,
We're moving, Hope.
You got four hours
to pack up whatever
you and Lizzie care about.

What?
I say.
What?

We're getting the hell
outta here,
Momma says.

I don't need
that woman spying on us.

But she's my friend,
I say.

I don't give a
damn who she is,
Momma says.

I don't want to go,
I say.

Momma throws things
into boxes and suitcases and
pillowcases
and even pots and pans.
She's packing us up.

No, no, no,
I think, but
I say,
I like it here.
This is our place.

We have to be here
for when Liz
comes back.

Momma doesn't listen.
She just packs.
And storms around.

I think about
Miss Freeman.

Her babysitting us
when we were little.
Her being there
when Daddy didn't come home.
Her watching me and Liz
from her picture window
to make sure we were safe.
Making us dinner.
Checking on me.
Now she knows something.
Something that has scared
my momma.

I don't want to go,
I say.

But just like that,
we're gone
from this
little old house
I have known my whole
life.

Gone from my
shared room
and the smells of Lizzie
and the kittens out back
and our club.

Stuffing the mattresses
in the trunk
of our car,
tying things in
and on
and over
like

The Beverly Hillbillies

and like that,
we're gone from Miss Freeman

who knows something.

71.

We end up
moving closer
to Mari.
In a two-bedroom trailer set up
on concrete blocks
not that far from the Wal-Mart
not even a half mile
from our old
home.

We won't be here long,
Momma says.

This place isn't permanent,
Momma says.

That fat busybody
drove us
from our home,
Momma says.

She clicks her tongue.
This place is so small,
she says,
looking at the

fake kitchen cabinets
and the orange carpeting
and the green linoleum,
that I will need you outta here
when I bring my friends
over.

All right,
I say,
hating the idea
that we have moved
on my Liz.

72.

Last night,
after I was settled
in from the move,
I had another
nightmare.

It's one that
haunts me.

Creatures
come from outer space.
They look just like people
only they're covered
in brown fur.
And they're blind.
They snap long whips
to see where people are.

In my dream they
always get close,
but they never can quite catch me,
which is good,
because then I can warn people
aliens are here on earth,
coming to get us.

I jerk awake
and remember the diary.

I know where it is.
I know
where Liz's kept it hid all along.

I turn on my side
and stare at my sister's mattress
left propped next
to the wall
because Momma didn't
have the time to
set things up
for Lizzie.
She ain't here is she?
Momma said.
So why should I do it?
I couldn't
argue with that.

My hands shake
and I'm not sure
if it's the dream
making me feel this way

or the little book.
But
something leaves me with
cold guts.

Think of something else,
I say to myself.
My voice sounds so loud
in the semi-dark
of this new room
with less of a promise
of Liz
than the last.

And lonely, too.

73.

A month and a half
before Liz
went to the hospital,
Momma said to her,
Let's paint this room
of yours any way you
want.
We'll decorate it
your choice.
What colors do you choose?

It's my room too,
I said.

Butter yellow and olive green,
Liz said.

Momma ignored me.

Butter yellow and olive green it is,
she said.

It's my room too,
I said again,
feeling rumpled inside.

I'd like purple and . . .

Did I ask you?
Momma said.
Did I?
Keep your mouth shut.

I wanted to be mad
at Liz,
but she had been looking sad
for a few days now
and the butter yellow and olive green
idea
seemed to cheer her up some.

Is that okay with you?
she asked,
when we walked out to the car.
I can change colors if you want.

I looked at her sad eyes.

No,
I said.
I think it'll be fine.

Momma bought spray paint,
three different cans
from the hardware store,
one yellow,
one green,
one white
to mix with the other
two.

Then she said,
Your choice of restaurants,
Lizzie girl.
What place do you choose?

Bahama Joe's?
Liz said,
like a question.

Perfect,
Momma said.
And she laughed a light laugh.

And that's where we went.
A seafood place,
though I hate seafood

and Momma and Liz
both know that.

It's fine,
I said,
I'll get hush puppies and coleslaw.
Maybe clam chowder, too.

But it wasn't really okay.
I felt grouchy inside,
bugged that Momma chose Liz
for everything.
I couldn't think one time
Momma ever let me
pick a place to eat.
Not one.

Momma and Liz
each got the all-you-can-eat
fried catfish dinner.

Right before we were ready to go,
Momma said,
I'm having company,
he'll be visiting tomorrow night.

I'm supposed to spend
the night at Mari's,
I said.

Liz didn't say anything,
just looked at her plate
and her face seemed to fade.
Even her freckles.

You can go,
Momma said
to me.
Since Liz picked out
where we ate and
the colors for your room,
you can spend the
night with Mari.

Liz looked at me a second
then at the big fish tank
that's part of Bahama Joe's
decoration.

When we got home,
Momma only painted one

piece of furniture—a bookshelf—
yellow.

It looked crappy,
because she chose
spray paint,
and she tried to mix it,
then she quit.

And in bed that night,
with the room smelling
so that we had to open
all the windows,
Liz whispered to me,
I think it's best you go away
tomorrow.

I was sleepy and still a little
unhappy about the day.

Can I get in bed with you?
Liz said.
Her voice sounded broken.

I almost said no,

but I changed my mind.

Yeah, if you don't hog the covers,
I said.

I won't,
Liz said,
and slid into
bed next to me
almost without
moving.

74.

I wish Ian could come over,
I say to Mari.
We're on a first-name
basis with Ian
St. Clair.

We stand in the Wal-Mart
looking for hair bleach
(for me, too!)
and talking about
Mari's upcoming boy/girl party.
A party Liz might
have come to,
if she wasn't still in
the hospital.

That would be so cool,
Mari says.
She looks at me with
her big brown eyes.

She has the
prettiest eyes in all of Florida.

Me and Mari stand silent,

me thinking
just how great it would be
if anybody really cute
showed up.

A voice comes over
the speaker saying M&M's
are on sale
on aisle five.

We'd have to take turns
dancing with him,
Mari says,
then she looks at the bleach.

Your hair is a lot blonder, Hope,
Mari says,
after a quiet moment,
and if I'm going to match
you I'll need something
strong.
And light.
I think I'll go with Buttercup Yellow.
What about you?

I'm not thinking
about bleaching my hair.
I am wondering about
anyone who is cute that
might be at Mari's
boy/girl party.

Hope, what about you?
Mari says.

I decide right then,
why not?
I like this red,
I say,
and pull a box out
with an auburn-haired girl
on the cover.
Her hair is near
the color of Liz's,
only shinier.
And the girl smiles big,
too.

Turning all that natural blond red,
Mari says,

like she's her mother all the sudden,
and like this wasn't her idea.
Then
Mari grabs me tight by the arm.

Isn't this exciting?
she says.

And it is,
till the coloring is said
and done.

75.

Oh no.

That's my first reaction.
Then Mari's.
And her mother's, too.
Who'da thunk we'd
all say the same thing?

My momma says,
Girl, you look like a whore.
What in the hell were you thinking?

Then she drives off
to meet a friend,
laughing and shaking her head,
leaving me to take care of
my own problems.

My hair
is the color of an
orange sunset.

Mari's is worse.
She does look like
a yellow flower,

just like the box said
she would.

But this isn't a pretty flower.
No, this one is almost dead.
Awful.
Ugly.
With purple undertones
that have gone gray.

Thank goodness
it's summer
and there's no school
for another couple of months.

But there is the boy/girl party.
And I can't go looking like this.

Soon as Momma pulls out
of the driveway
I start looking for money.

Clairol has done me wrong.
Maybe L'Oréal can set things straight.

I dial Mari's number.

76.

My mother,
Mari says
when she picks up the phone,
is still squealing at me
like a stuck pig.

I can hear her in the background.

Well, my momma,
I say,
called me a bunch of ugly names.

Mari lets out
a guffaw.

I'm riding my bike over to the A & P,
I say.
I gotta get this hair back
to normal.
Maybe black dye will work.
You wanna go?

Good idea,
Mari says.
How about if I ask

my grandmother to take us.
She's here now.

Mari lowers her voice
and says,
Guess what?
She didn't notice a thing.
All she's been
doing is arguing with
my mother.

My nana is tucked away
in Miami.
She won't know anything
about my hair until our next family
reunion,
which is at the beginning of September.
Momma is already practicing a song
she wants us to sing that day.

Grandmother says she will take us,
Mari says.

Okay,
I say.

And true to her word,
Mari comes driving up
in an antique,
light blue
Chevrolet,
with her ancient,
wrinkled granny sitting
behind the wheel.

That little old woman
can just see over
the steering wheel
and she's sitting on
the Orlando phone book
to boot.
Her voice, though, can rattle leaves
loose from their trees.

Shake a leg, Hope,
she hollers at me.
The lights on this old thing
have been giving me fits.

I run
to the car with

dollar bills
and a few quarters
and dimes
stuck in the pocket of
my shorts.

Thanks for taking us,
I say.

Mari's grandmother doesn't answer.
She never does.
Mari says it's
'cause the old lady can't hear
a thing and knows it,
so why and try and say anything?

Sunset oranges up the sky
with streaks of turquoise.

At the store
we hunt the dye/bleach aisle over,
trying to find something
that might work.

I decide to go darker

than my natural blond color.

Mari decides she is
going to go two-tone.

Her grandmother buys us
each a banana split
from Dairy Queen
and we start for home.

Things are fine for a while.

By now it's dark
and the streetlights flicker on
and brighten up the
gray-colored road.

For sure,
nighttime in Florida
can feel darker than it is.
Maybe it's the humidity,
or the trees stretching
over the road,
or maybe
it is just the thoughts

sitting in the back of my head
about my sister.

I'm squished in the front,
with Mari
between me and
her grandmother.

The thirty-minute ride takes
us an hour and a half
because the car lights
keep flashing off and on.

Every time the lights go out,
the old woman weaves
over the dotted line
into the wrong lane,
to the side of the road,
scaring even the ditch,
I'm sure.

Grandmother,
Mari yells,
you are gonna kill us dead.
Pull over.

Her grandmother parks on the side
of the road, and we wait
for the car lights to brighten up some
and send out a weak bit of light so
we can get on home.

It's hot outside
and there's no breeze
coming in through the open
windows.

The mosquitoes eat us alive.
They must be attracted
by my pounding heart.
Almost losing your life
several times over can
really make the blood flow.

I'll get out here,
I say,
a mile from home.
I can't die
with my hair looking like this.

Chicken,
Mari says.
But I laugh at her and climb out
of the car, slamming
the door shut.

I jog,
taking shortcuts through
empty fields,
passing houses,
keeping to the edge
of our dirt road.

Once I get to the trailer
I set to work
putting my hair back to normal.

77.

I find out three things
this evening:

1. There are worse things
   than staying with your best
   friend and her grandmother
   in a death-trap Chevrolet,
   weaving or no weaving.

2. L'Oréal doesn't work any
   better than Clairol.
   and

3. Buttercup Yellow doesn't
   work for me, either.

78.

Momma comes in
to where I sit that night,
folded in a beanbag chair,
reading *Heck Superhero*.

She's been watching TV all day.
She looks nervous,
something I don't see from her often.

Hey,
she says.
I just got a call
from the hospital.

I go all cold in my guts
and the freeze
seems to leak through
my whole body.

Liz?
I say,
though my tongue feels
thin as a slice of ham.
Is it Liz?

Has she managed it?
Has she done
what she had set out to do?

Is my sister dead?

She's okay,
Momma says,
though there's not
a lot of improvement.
She's talking a bit.
Up and around.

Momma touches at her hair
that she's pulled back with
little girl barrettes.
Pink plastic ones.
Some days she dresses like this,
in blue jeans and baby clothes,
like she's not a mother
or
a prostitute.

You figure out where
that diary is of hers?

Momma says,
her voice lean.
I seen her writing in it.
You know where it is?

I shake my head.
At least I am not voicing the lie.

You sure?
Momma says.

Haven't laid eyes on it,
I say.
And that's the truth.

I know,
in my brain,
where it is.
But for sure I've left it there,
in my memory and
in its hiding place
on purpose.
It seems a piece of something
I'm afraid to look at
and I have a feeling Liz

wants it left where it is.
At least for now.

Well,
Momma says,
her psychiatrist wants
to talk to **you** now.
And with your
hair looking like
that.

I put a hand to my head.

Her words of seeing the doctor
send a streak
through me that feels like electricity.
I jolt up.

Why me?
I say.
I don't know nothing.

And I think,
Except where the diary is.

Momma gives a tiny smile,
one that I almost can't see
though I notice her hands shake.
Has she heard my thoughts?

You have to talk to him,
Momma says.
I told him no,
but he insisted.

Now I am scared through
and through.
Will I end up with my sister,
drugged and sleeping most of the time,
wanting to be dead?
Will Momma complain
about my costs too?

I push myself
out of the chair and toss my book aside.
Heck, Spence, and Marion
are gonna have to
wait till my nerves settle before
I can finish reading about them.

I'm going for a walk,
I tell Momma,
then take off.

Up the sand and rock
driveway I go,
slapping at mosquitoes.

Why does this guy want to see me?
Why?
I haven't done anything.
And I don't know why
Liz didn't want to live.

The moon rides high in the sky,
washing the fruit trees
and pines
and oaks
I pass with
a fine white light.

Full moon means werewolf,
I say
and a mosquito

answers me with a sting
on the cheek.

79.

Momma drives, hands clenched,
to the steering wheel.

Listen up,
she says
without giving me
a chance to speak.

We Chapmans
stick together.
We don't tell
nothing about our
lives.
Not to doctors or nurses.

Momma pauses long enough
to get a cigarette
lit.
She draws in a deep
breath of smoke
then sends it out
through her nose.

When she speaks
again, smoke leaks

from her mouth
with the words,
Or with neighbors.
We keep our secrets
tight.

She looks at me
side-eyed, not quite
taking her eyes off the
road and says,
You understand, Hope?

I'm quiet a long minute.

Do you?

Yes, ma'am,
I say, watching palm
fronds and pine trees
zip past the car
window.
Yes, ma'am, I understand.

And I do.

I understand that
Momma is hiding
something to do with
my sister,
Lizzie.

80.

The psychiatrist
looks just like some guy right
offa the TV.
Little glasses,
pudgy belly,
even a beard.

What I don't expect is his office.
No couch to lie down on.
Instead three beige
easy chairs circle a coffee table
that is empty except for
a box of tissues.

Dollhouses,
hand painted,
model cars,
and rocket ships
fill the shelves.
Lots of framed pictures
drawn by kids
cover the walls.
Paint-by-numbers, too.

I see this all
as I stand near the doorway.

Mrs. Chapman,
the doctor says,
you can join us too.
Let's all meet together
for a few minutes.

Momma shakes her
head no.
I already spent plenty
of time in there,
she says.
You meet with Hope now.

Just for a few minutes,
he says.

I stand halfway between
them, holding up
the wall,
waiting.

But Momma, unlit

cigarette between her fingers,
just points at me
and says,
You remember
what I said, Hope.

Then Momma hightails it outta there,
shouting over her shoulder
she'll be back in less than an hour,
for me to be ready.

The doctor and I
look each other over.
He points to his
office with his whole
hand.

I'm Dr. Marino,
he says and
reaches to shake
with me
but I edge into
the room.

Sit down.

Get comfortable.

I want to laugh.
Get comfortable?
You said that in
a shrink's office?
What's he been smoking
to think I can get
comfortable.
I sit my butt
on the edge of a chair.

We look at each other
for a moment,
him over the top
of those glasses,
and he says,
So, Hope,
how are you?

I shrug.

I know that feeling,
he says, and then,
Do you know why you're here?

296

You're making me?
I say.

He grins.
Settles into a chair
so that we are almost knee-to-knee.
I move back
in the seat.

I look past him,
at a painting of what looks
like people with their heads cut off.
Tell me
about you, Hope.

Me?
I say, surprised.

Absolutely,
he says,
with this smile
in his eyes like
he wants to
know me.

At the end of the
forty-five minutes,
when I have
told Dr. Marino
about me
and Mari
and my dad being gone
and Lizzie leaving too
(and yes,
even a little about Momma
and her job),
he says,
Next time,
let's talk about
you and Lizzie.

I nod.

Walking out to the
car with Momma,
who asks over and over
to tell all I told the doctor,
I think two things.

One
how did that all come
out of me?
Two
Momma is not going
to be happy about
me spending all that
money chatting
about who
I am.

What a bunch of shit,
Momma says.
He coulda saved me
a helluva lotta
money if you had just
written your life story down
and sent it to him
with a Forever
stamp.

81.

Our second session
goes like this:

Hope, your mother
will be with us today.

I knew this.
Momma ranted the whole
way from Ormond
to the hospital
about the wasted money
wasted gas
wasted time.

I knew Momma
would be there
and the idea of it scared me.
Momma listening.
Me working hard to
guard my words.

Dr. Marino settles
us in his office.

We're uncovering a mystery here,

he says,
and Momma
lets a sound out of her nose
that is something
like a snort.

Dr. Marino ignores her,
looks right at me.
A mystery about Elizabeth
and why
she would want to
kill herself.

Now, Hope,
I've talked with your mother
and we have discussed this.

I glance at Momma
and her eyes bore
into me.

We're all worried about Elizabeth,
Dr. Marino says.

And I think,

Yes, I am. Yes,
I
am.

Dr. Marino put his fingertips
together, then rests his chin
on the pointers.
He waits, expecting.

And soon I am thinking, I
I do know where the diary is.
I do know.
I do
know.
I do.
I
do.
Like something
from *The Wizard of Oz* movie
and the Cowardly
Lion.

Your mother is here
because this is
tough stuff

we're going to talk about.
Okay?

I don't look at Momma.

When people change so much,
change so fast,
he says to me
and Momma,
like Elizabeth has,
that many times means
something has happened
in that person's life.
In this case,
in Elizabeth's
life.

Momma shifts in her seat.
When I look at her,
she looks
back at me like
I was the one who
made the appointment
with Dr. Marino.

So we know,
Dr. Marino says,
that something
must have changed
in Elizabeth's life,
for her to try and
kill herself.

He leans forward in his chair.

Your mother told me, Hope, that this
started with your sister
three months ago,
maybe a little more.

What?
I say.

That Elizabeth
tried to kill herself several times.

Several times?
I say.
It feels like hands
have pushed me

down in the chair
and will not let
me up.
Several?
I say.

I look at Momma.

Tears crawl down
her cheeks.

Several, Momma?

You didn't know?
Dr. Marino says.

I shake my head.
I didn't know,
I say.
I didn't know more than once.
More than the gun.
The words somehow
make it
past the fist
in my throat.

But you knew later?
he says.

I stopped her,
I say,
I stopped her before she
came here,
I stopped her
from leaving us for
good.

Guilt courses through
me so I feel it on
my skin, like
I could scrape it
away with my fingernails,
if I dug hard
enough.

Several times is serious,
he says.

I told you,
Momma says,
her voice strained

in the office air,
that Liz is sensitive.

That's true,
I say,
and I think of
her crying at night.

Dr. Marino nods.
But even sensitive people
don't try to kill
themselves without a
reason. So
three times is
serious.

One time is serious,
I say.

Momma laughs and says,
Even without
a degree
she figured
that
one out.

It's like Dr. Marino
doesn't hear Momma.

Why might she
want to end her life?
he says.

I try to say,
Not sure,
but my voice squeezes
out like maybe I
am sure.

Squeezes out
like I *do* know
where the diary is.

I do know.
I do.

And then I get this memory
of Liz standing alone on the porch,
watching me ride away on my bike,
to Mari's house.

And I think of that damn diary again.
That's what Momma has
been calling it for days now,
That Damn Diary.

And on the
inside of me
I look away.

At the end
of the forty-five minutes
Dr. Marino says,
You know, Hope,
if you think of anything
that might help us figure
this mystery out, you can call me.
Anytime, day or night.
I live in Winter Park.
Kyle Marino.
Here's my number,
and he scratches it down.
Call me at home if you need to.

Okay,
I say.

And my voice
has less weight than
the sticky note he's handed
me.

I fold the number up tiny
and shove it deep
into my pocket.

And if you think of anything that's,
you know, unusual,
you can tell me next time you visit.

He stands,
shakes hands with
Momma
and me.

Next time nothing,
Momma says
under her breath.

I start from the room,
then turn back.
I touch the cool jamb

with the palm of my hand.
From the front of the office
I can smell coffee.

In my memory
Lizzie stands
alone
on the porch
watching after
me.

She doesn't like to be alone,
I say.
And she cries lots at night.

Dr. Marino nods.
Maybe he knows that
already.

82.

Don't give him information,
Momma says,
driving home fast,
unless he asks first.

The windows are down
and ocean smell
fills the car.

A summer storm heads
toward us fast
the sky blooming
with black clouds.
Before
we have gone even a mile more
rain hits
the car like gunshots.

He has asked,
I say. And think,
Like a gunshot.

83.

Liz has been gone from home almost the whole summer.

84.

And
I do know.
Where That.
Diary.
Is.

85.

Once,
a **long** time ago,
Momma
took us to the river.

I was little,
just learning to swim.
Momma fastened an orange
Styrofoam bubble around
my waist to keep me afloat.

Then she sat
in the hot sun with
Lizzie right close to her.
Liz played in the sand
in her underpanties,
half a butt cheek showing.

Momma rubbed olive oil
on her skin to brown herself.

I love my babies,
Momma said.
Run into the water, Hope.

I did,
getting just my toes wet,
then my feet,
and finally plunging
in to my waist.
The bubble popped me up.

I played that afternoon,
sharing my bubble with Liz,
until a rainstorm came.
It pattered on the face of the river.
Momma and me and Liz huddled under
a towel.
The wet sand smelled good,
like something hot and fresh.

Lookit out there,
Momma said.

Where?
Lizzie said.

Out there on the river,
Momma said.
It's a family of snakes.

I stood from under
the towel letting the
raindrops beat on my skin
and I looked for the snakes.

At last I saw them,
swimming toward shore,
three of them.

Three like us, Momma,
I said.

Yes, three like us,
Momma said.
A momma with her two babies.
And they're coming this way.

Momma was quiet a moment,
then she said,
Moccasins.
My God, they're moccasins.
Run, Hope.
Run, Liz.

The snakes must have

seen us by then. They
turned in our direction.

Momma didn't pick a thing up.
Not the umbrella,
not the towel she sat on.
Not even that sweet smelling
olive oil.

She just ran,
leaving me and Liz behind.

Wait,
Liz hollered after her.
Wait for us.
Liz grabbed
me by the hand
but all the sudden
I couldn't even move.

Baby,
Lizzie said.
Come on.

She tried to pick me up,

but that bubble
made it hard.

Now the snakes were
on land and coming fast,
so fast,
and I couldn't move.

Come on, Liz, Hope,
Momma called.
She was a good ways away.

The rain kept coming down
all silver looking.
It ran in my eyes.

Liz!
Just leave Hope there,
Momma called.
Her voice was scared.
Leave her and run to me.

Liz grabbed the belt
of the bubble and
pulled me along,

like you might a pup
that didn't want to follow.

Liz screamed,
Hope.

Now the snakes were so close
I could see their eyes.
One opened its mouth
and I saw the white cotton.

Run,
Liz screamed at me.
And somehow
I could move.

We ran

together.

86.

Damn it!
Momma says when
we are almost home
from our joint
visit to Dr. Marino.

She pulls the car over.
The rain has blinded us.
The windshield wipers do nothing.
Steam fills up the car.

I write *Liz*
on my window,
then open it
a crack to let
cigarette smoke
out of the car
and a bit of rain
and air in.

I don't get it,
Momma says.

I glance at her.
Ooh,

she is mad.
Madder than a hornet.

More visits?
Why you?

I shrug.
Not sure,
I say.
I stare out the car window
and touch my pocket
where the number is.

You thinking
of killing yourself too?
Have you told him that?
Momma squeezes the
steering wheel,
smashes out a half-smoked
cigarette,
lights another,
blows smoke
in my direction.

No!
I say.

We wait in silence
till the rain calms
then
Momma drives home fast,
her teeth clenching away
at nothing but air.

87.

If you think of anything that's,
you know, unusual . . .
Where is that diary?
Run!
I close my eyes to these thoughts.

Something good.
Think anything good.

Something
must have changed
in Elizabeth's life,
for her to try and
kill herself.

Three times?
Three times?
Three times?

Oh dear.
Oh no.
I know this.
I know this.
Crying in my head.
Crying in my head.

No!
Think of something else.
Hope!

Why my name?
Why is she calling me?

88.

Right before the end of school,
right when Liz
started her night crying,
Momma
got Liz a little black pup,
all wiggly with joy.

Lizzie named him Midnight.

If I get you this,
Momma said,
will you stop all the nighttime
crying?

Yes, Momma,
she said.

We stood in the animal shelter,
poopy smells enough to coat
your tongue
listening to animals bark and cry.
Right in front of us was the
fat black pup,
not a lick of white hair on it.

Sure is cute,
I said
and
held my nose.

Sure is,
Liz said.
She crouched over,
her hair falling forward,
and pushed her fingers
through the wire of the cage,
letting that little thing
lick at her.

I stood beside Lizzie,
my leg touching her side.

He loves me, Hope.
See that?
she said.
She gave me a kind-of glance
and I saw this spark in her eyes.

I said,
Yeah, I see he does.

Momma bought
that little ol'
pup.

Lizzie and me,
we both loved Midnight
all the way home,
sweet baby that he was.

That night and every night
for a little bit
it happened like this:

Lizzie climbed into bed
with that dog.
The two of them would lie
there and before long, once
all the lights were out, Liz
would start her bawling.

It was small crying at first,
then it got louder
until some nights,
I dreamed of an airplane

flying close
to my ear.

There were evenings when
I felt as scared as my sister
sounded.
Her voice frightened me,
crying out
like that.
Made me want to bawl
myself
alongside her.

Momma would close me
and Lizzie out there in our room,
locking us in
with Midnight.

What is it, Liz? What?
I asked.
Why you crying?
Why?
And she'd shake her
head and hold that dog
tight.

Let me turn on the radio,
I'd say, or a CD.

Sometimes it would help,
sometimes not.

Come get in bed with me,
I'd say.
You can even bring Midnight,
bad breath and
all.

Sometimes it would help,
sometimes not.

Let me tell you a funny story,
I'd say.

Sometimes it would help,
sometimes not.

And once Midnight moved
into our house, he cried
along with Liz.

Please,
why do you cry at night?
I asked,
tired out.

Life is different in the day,
Liz would say
in the mornings,
her eyes red from the
weeping
and dark circles
sweeping toward
her cheekbones.

I don't think Momma
meant to run Midnight over.
I really don't.
I saw her eyes when
the dog cried out and
Lizzie came running
to scoop him up.
There was as much surprise
in Momma's eyes
as there was sadness in
Liz's.

Momma didn't get out of the
car, though. Just looked
at me, face all squinched up
and said,
Hope, throw him
over the fence
in that high grass
or bury him out where
we burn the garbage.

And as she pulled away she said,
At least things is gonna be
quieter around here.   .

But I heard the shakiness
in my momma's voice,
even over Liz's weeping.

89.

You seen them damn painted horses?
Momma says a few days later.
She's gone back to the old house,
a couple of times
looking through the things
we left behind
for that diary of
Lizzie's.

What horses?
I say,
scrubbing out the kitchen sink
whilst Momma strums
her guitar.
She likes the trailer kept
neat
even when she makes
the messes.

Them damn things is
what Lizzie makes in his office,
Momma says.
Talks to him while
she glues that stuff together.

I remember the shaky
lines painted down the
sides of a palomino,
the eye decals glued on crooked.

I'm in the wrong business,
Momma says,
and she sets the guitar down
with a musical thump.

I should be working with crazies,
Momma says.
I could instruct someone
to put together a Model T.
A three-hundred-and-fifty
dollar plastic piece of crap.
We'd be living
high off the hog,
just like he does.

Then she is gone,
stomping from the room
and out the trailer.
I hear the car start
and roar away.

When I rinse the sink,
I see my hands shake.

Good grief
get ahold of yourself,
Hope,
I think.

I hurry myself along.
I sweep,
wipe down the fridge,
damp mop the floor,
then dust Momma's little
collection of salt and pepper
shakers.

The whole time I work
I bite at my bottom lip
until
it bleeds.

Then I move out of the
kitchen in slow motion
out the door
away from here.

I walk like a Seminole Indian
might, my feet not
even making a sound.
Maybe not even touching
the ground
I'm so quiet.

I walk,
checking every once in a while,
over my shoulder.

90.

Who does all the pictures?
I say.

Another visit with the doctor.
Dr. Marino looks at me over
the top of his glasses.
A habit of his,
I guess.

He says,
Children I've worked with.
Clients.

I get up
and make my way
around the room,
looking at the drawings.

Lots of war.
Crying people.
Blood.
One rainbow picture
with a whole family standing under it.

I check that one for

Lizzie's name.
Carlos, it says.

What makes you feel safe, Hope?
he says.
I sit now.
It's cold in here.
The carpet's too soft
and the lights are too bright.

I say,
What do you mean?

You know,
he says.
Where do you feel secure?

I think.
With Liz.
With Mari.
In school.

Air-conditioning
fills the room with
a low buzz.

How about at home?
Do you feel safe there?

I shrug.
I guess so,
I say.

With your mom?
he asks

At first I can't say anything.
It's not like Momma hits us
or anything.
But still.
Things have changed.
Changed.
This move, for one.

Before
when it was
all of us
Daddy, Momma, me, and Lizzie.
Then
it was
good.

Great, even. Liz has told
me so.
And I remember
from the pictures.

Sure,
I say now.
I can't look him in the eye.
Yeah, sure
I feel safe with
her.

That afternoon,
all the long way home with Momma,
I notice something about
me.

I watch her
side-eyed.
And when she lights
up a cigarette,
I flinch.

91.

I've been sitting
in Dr. Marino's office
for nearly fifteen minutes
and neither one of us has
said much of anything.

He's asked me
again
to think what has scared
Lizzie so much
she wants to
die.

I'm trying to think
what I should say.
I come up with a dream.
Not the alien one.
This one's different.

Maybe things were
haunted at our place,
I say.

I'm not sure why I say this.
I don't believe that one bit.

All the crying Liz did
would scare away the
worst ghoul.

Haunted?
Dr. Marino says.

I tip my head, thinking.
The crying,
I say.

What crying?

He knows about Lizzie's crying
all night
but this one is different.
This one
is dreams.

I heard it at night
at the other place,
I say.
This soft stuff.
Like a kitten or something.

But the kittens, I know,
are all gone now. Not one
left.

Dr. Marino takes off his
glasses and wipes at the
greasy spots on his nose.
He squeezes his eyes shut tight.

Tell me,
he says.

It happened a lot
right before school
got out,
I say.
These crying dreams I had.
I thought it was something
outside, but it must be in
my head.
And it didn't
happen all the time.
Only once in a while,
when I slept alone.
When Liz slept with Momma.

343

Dr. Marino says nothing.
He does nothing.

I asked Momma,
I say,
and she said it was me dreaming.
She said she was trying to
keep Liz quiet
at least once in a while
by having her in her bed.

In your mother's bed?
Dr. Marino says.
His glasses are back on now,
and his face has changed,
like he's onto something
like a little bulb
small as a night-light bulb,
has gone on behind the skin
of his face.

And what do you think?
he says,
like I might really know.

That Momma's right,
I say, shrugging.
It was me dreaming.
Hasn't happened,
not even one time,
in the trailer.

(Neither has Lizzie's crying with me.)

All at once I'm caught
off guard with
the feeling that washes
over me
during this crying dream
and what I have
just said.
It's cold, this feeling,
and prickly
and the hair
on back of my neck
stands up straight.
My ankle joints
freeze.

We're both quiet

for a long moment
and then Dr. Marino says,
You say the dreams have
stopped now that Elizabeth
is gone?

I would nod,
but my neck feels stuck
in place.

92.

I have it.
Went and got it.
Brought it back.

Even though
Momma isn't home I
stick that old diary
under my shirt and
head to my room.

I am so afraid,
I think I can't
take a step.

If Momma found out
I've known all along . . .

if she knew about
the breaking and entering
though no one has moved
into our old place
and Momma has gone
there herself before
for the diary

and for things
we need
like a couple of pots
and sofa pillows.

If Momma knew . . .
Just say,
I speak to myself
as I walk fast to my room,
just say that you
found it
when we were moving.

Say that you were planning
on giving it to her.
Not that you walked
back for it.
Not that you dragged
cinder blocks into
the house
until there were
enough to peek
(and then saw it
wasn't in the

attic
which meant one big ol' thing.)

In the doorway of my bedroom
I stop.
Now what?
Now what?
Now what?

My mind plays the words fast
so they become one big word
one long word that won't end.

Nowwhatnowwhatnowwhat?

Where do I hide this thing?
I'm whispering,
panic clawing up
my throat.

I move all over my room, looking
for the right place,
the safe place.

And for some reason,
with that diary,
I know there's no safe place.
None.

93.

In the bookshelf
the diary
is so short that it stands out
like a whale on the beach.

Under my mattress is too
obvious a hiding place.
My drawers,
too easy a target.

Is that why Liz
hid the diary
at Miss Freeman's
place?

(I need the diary,
Miss Freeman,
I said, when I
walked across the street
to her place
because
that had to be where it was.

The doctor,
Dr. Marino,

said for me to
get it,
I said.

All right then,
Miss Freeman said.

She let me in the living room
with the plastic flowers, doilies
on all the furniture arms,
and three pictures of
Jesus,
one of Him
wearing a crown of thorns.

Miss Freeman lumbered to the back
of her house
and when
she returned,
holding the diary in a
Ziploc bag,
my stomach lurched
right into my heart,
knocking it out of place some,
I think.

Your sister said, Hide it,
so I did,
Miss Freeman said.
Liz-baby said you'd
be by to get it,
maybe.

She did?
I said.
It felt like needles
pricked my face.

She did,
Miss Freeman said.

She leaned close and said,
I didn't read it, Hope.
Wasn't right for
me to read it.

I noticed we looked
eye-to-eye.
When had I grown as
tall as her?

And you're okay?
she said,
handing me the diary,
small
and pink
and old-looking,
tucked in that Ziploc.

Miss Freeman touched my hand.
Her fingers were
damp with sweat
and soft as a
marshmallow.

I'm okay,
I said.
Sort of.)

At home
I wedge the book
in the crack between
what will be Liz's
mattress
and the old wooden frame.

Thank goodness it's so small.
It fits like this was
the hiding place always.

Then I run from the house
so I won't be there when
Momma comes back,
my heart pounding in my throat
like I swallowed a fish.

I walk into town
fingering leftover change
in my pocket.

The same way me and Liz did before.
Only now the trip is
painful,
like the fish hasn't moved
and isn't going to.

When I get to
the Dairy Queen,
I buy myself a Dilly Bar,
cherry flavored,
Liz's favorite.

Lizzie,
I think.
I'm tired and I'm scared.

As good as it tastes,
that ice cream,
hard cherry-flavored shell,
does nothing
to erase the sick,
sick
feeling of the diary
out of its safe place.

And me still having to read it.

94.

Okay,
Mari says,
Hope, you are in
charge of the party games.

Party games?
I say.
What kind of party games?

I've never done anything
like this before.
Never even **been** to a party
like this before.

We sit at a small
round table
by the pool. Mari's
mom and dad
stand at the left-hand
corner of her yard
deciding where to put
a gazebo
and a rose garden.

You know what kind

of games,
Mari says,
waving her hand around
like I really **do** know.
Like . . . ,
Mari pauses,
because, just
as I suspected,
she has no idea what kind of games
either.

Oh you know,
she says, waving her hand
again. Then she starts
listing food for the party
out loud.

Tacosandsalsaandguacamole
andcandyandsodaandachocolate
fountainwithbananasandstrawberries
andgrahamcrackerstodip,
she says in one breath.

Good,

I say.
Eating can be one of
our games.

Mari rolls her eyes at me.

This has got to be
the best party ever,
she says,
so that Robbie notices
me and Jace notices
you.

Mari's hair is pink
and purple
today, covering
the yellow purple gray of two days
ago. I
am sure that Robbie
will notice her.

And maybe not Jace,
but maybe **Alex**
will see me,

really see me,
dyed hair
and all.

The thought makes my
heart flutter.

You are in charge of the games,
Mari says again.
She taps her chin
with a pencil
before pressing the lead
to her tongue.
Make sure they
are kissing games.

Right,
I say,
wondering if I can find
kissing games
on the Internet.

95.

I do.

Suck and blow,
I say, looking over
my shoulder
at Mari whose list
has grown one and a half
pages long.

What?
Mari says,
and then she
laughs her face off.

It's a kissing game,
I say, my face going
hot.

I gotta keep this party
PG–13,
Mari says.
No sucking.
No blowing.

She laughs again and her hair

catches in an evening breeze and waves
like flowers nodding.

No,
I say,
I said it's a kissing game.

Mari raises her eyebrows.
One is half shaved-off.
Don't ask me why.
I don't know.
It was gone when I got here.

You use playing cards,
I say,
sucking a card
so it stays on your lips
and passing it to someone else
without touching it
with your hands.

And?
she says.

And,

I say,
if you want to kiss
that person you're passing the card
to, you just let it drop.

My face is still
red but Mari seems
too busy to notice.

Sounds like a good one,
she says.
Better than spin the bottle.

For a moment
I imagine me
and Alex.

Me and Alex.

Just a playing card
separating us.
Would I feel
the warmth of his lips
through that bit of
cardboard?

The thought is too much.

I better go,
I say.
I best be alone with
my thoughts
so Mari doesn't
see me
all embarrassed and ask
what I'm thinking.

She expects me to be
with Jace Nelson.
And I can't tell her
that seeing Alex
makes my heart thrum.

96.

Wouldn't you know it?
Mari says,
when I get to her house
the next day.

Know what?
I say.

I can hear the party going
on in the back by the pool.
My first boy-girl party.
My hands sweat.

Is everybody here?

Yes,
she says.
Then Mari grabs me by the arm.
Guess what?
I started my period this afternoon
after we finished
decorating.

Oooh sorry,

I say,
meaning it.

Can you believe my luck?
she says.

Well, we didn't plan any swimming,
I say.
Just dancing by the pool.

I walk slow with my friend,
feeling sorry for her
and glad that it's not me
in her situation.

Outside, evening is coming full-on,
the sun sinking fast,
casting last bits of light at us.

AFI's newest album
plays from the stereo.
Mari and I walk out and I see
everyone in two groups.
The boys near the food.
The girls near the CD player.

None of this boy-girl
separating thing,
Mari says
in a loud voice.
Let's play spin the bottle.

A few people groan,
but they all look interested.

Mari arranges us in a circle.
Cathy Simmons and her sister
Jennifer giggle together until
Mari sticks Alex Cain
in between them.

She puts me and Jace Nelson
together, then Robbie Thorne.

Standing there in the circle,
like the center of a flower,
the party not even going on,
she motions to Jeff Ingold
and Laurel Stowe,
and last of all,
Bryan McGuire.

Mari holds out her arms
and then like maybe she's
announcing the Olympics
she says,
Let the party begin.
And laughs.

Robbie grins as Mari
comes to sit by him.

Then he says,
pointing crotch level on her,
Lookit right there.

Robbie is from Georgia
and his accent is thicker
than good cream.

What?
Mari says.
In the half-light
I see her face go blotchy red.

Lookit right there, Mari,

Robbie says pointing again,
crotch level.

Oh my gosh,
I think,
does he know she's on her period?
Does he **see** something?

My face begins to color too,
as everyone quiets down.
AFI stops singing
and everyone
everyone
looks at Mari.
There's silence
until an old Green Day song
comes on.

How dare you?
Mari says.
She smacks him a good one,
catching him on the ear
and the side of his head.
The slap makes a popping noise.

One of the guys lets
out a bark of a laugh
and Cathy says,
Mari!
like she can't believe it.

What?
Robbie says.
What? I was just telling
you there's something on your arm.
I think it's chocolate.
Jeez.

Chocolate?
she says.
Well, it better be,
Robbie Thorne.

Jeez,
he says again,
his hand on his face.

And with that accent,
I can't help but like him,

if only a little.

Alex
laughs like Robbie
deserves the slap.
Then he stares right at
me across the circle
so that I can't
quite swallow for fear
I'll make a *galunk*
sound.

Light-haired
brown-eyed Alex
lifts his chin
to me
and I look away for a moment
thinking my face
might burn away from pleasure.

When I look
back he's talking to
Cathy
and my stomach

deflates

until he glances at me again

and smiles.

97.

After the slap
after the eating
after the dancing
we gather
in the family room,
lights turned dim,
and sit in a circle.

I am across from
Alex,
not next to him
like I had hoped
and
there is so much
disappointment in my gut
that for a moment
I think,
Why should I be here?

On one side of me is Jace.
Mari is on the other.

Tell us the rules, Hope,
Mari says.

Everyone looks at me
and all the sudden
I feel shy.

But I force myself to talk
and I force myself to not
look at Alex as I
say the words,
Pass the card to the person
on your left
without using your hands,
just using your
breath and your lips.

Mari and I demonstrate,
me passing the card to her.
Then she turns to Robbie,
sucking on that card,
until his lips close in
and she drops it and
plants a big
smooch
right on his lips.

Oh!

She has so
much nerve!

The room breaks out
in whoops and hollers.

You don't **have**
to pass the card,
Mari says,
and she tucks her hair
behind her ears.

Well,
Robbie says,
his accent strong.
You've forgiven me?

Mari smiles.
Pass the card,
she says.

And the game starts.
The whole time
me
wishing

wishing
wishing
I could let the playing card
drop to the floor
between me
and Alex Cain.

98.

I stand at the door
with Mari
telling all her guests good-bye.

Alex
leans near,
touching my arm
as he passes
into the night.

His voice is low
and I can smell
Doublemint gum on his breath.

You should have passed me a card,
he says.

What?
I say
because I could not have heard
him right.

Night,
he says.
He raises his eyebrows at me.

And then he is gone.

Oh girl,
Mari says,
I think he likes you.

She lets out a laugh.

You think?
I say.
Really?

I think,
she says.
Really.

Right then I want
my Liz
so I can
tell her all about
Alex
and how his hair is
a little long and
how he's taller

than me
and skinny.

What would she say?

99.

Momma and me
surprise Liz one Saturday afternoon.
No one,
not even the doctors,
know we're coming for a visit.

A nurse leads us down the hall.
Liz is in Arts and Crafts,
she says.

Arts and crafts?
Liz is up for
Arts and Crafts?

Momma lets out a
disgusted sound
and says,
I picked me the
wrong career
in a whisper so loud
I know the nurse
hears.

We round the corner.

Momma hangs back,
outta sight.

The room is full of kids
working at tables.
There must be fifteen of them,
kids I mean.

I wonder,
Have you all tried to kill
yourselves? Is that why you
are here?

Liz isn't even the youngest.
But she *is* the prettiest.
I see her working.
She's doing something,
though I have no idea what.

From where
I stand
I see her hands shaking.

The nurse calls out Lizzie's name.

She sees me,
glances like
she's checking I'm alone,
and breaks out with a smile
as wide as our river.

Hey, Hope,
she says.
Come see what
I'm making for you.

She holds up a belt
and it wiggles a little,
like a snake caught by the tail.

I'm putting your initials on it,
she says.

I hurry to her
and grab her into a hug.
You're talking,
I say.
You're better!

I cannot believe this
change in my sister.
She smells like lotion
and the light in the room
is so bright.

You're better,
I want to say again,
I want to say,
How?
Why?
What happened?
but Lizzie
doesn't give me
the chance.

I press in the leather with this,
she says.
She holds up a metal tool
I don't recognize.

She looks tired,
yes.
Worn-out.

More thin than I've
ever seen
her.
But she's talking.
Standing
(though shaky)
up!

Then I can paint them.
What colors do you choose?

I clear my throat.
Your favorites,
I say, my voice caught
near the back of
my tongue.
Do butter yellow and olive green.

Oh, I have missed her.
Oh, I have missed my sister.
My real sister
not the shadow she was
before.

Lizzie girl,
Momma says,
coming from around the corner
fast as a bus.

I heard you talking,
she says.
I heard you talking to Hope.

Liz flinches.
Then
turns away.

Now, I heard you,
Momma says.
She walks fast to Liz,
who moves to a window
that's covered in mesh.
She drops the belt
and I run
to pick it up
to hand it back
to my real sister,

my real Lizzie.

But I don't
get the chance.

You can't fool me,
Momma says
and she is right
in Lizzie's face.

Momma,
I say,
wait.

But she can't hear
me, maybe.

Mrs. Chapman,
the nurse says.
It's best not to push her.

I watch without breathing.
No one in the room
says a word. Like they all
want to know

what will happen
now.

Be careful.

Hush, baby.
Shhhh.

Lizzie,
Momma says,
her hands like claws
though she doesn't
touch my sister.
But if she could,
why I wonder if
she'd scratch Liz's
eyes from her skull.
You gotta talk to me sometime.

Liz doesn't say a thing.
She just finds a chair.
Sits.
Her head bows
and she is
gone.

My real sister
is
gone.

You hear me?
Momma says and her voice gets loud.
She bends over Liz.
Her hands still claws.

Momma,
I say,
the words stuck
in my throat,
don't.

You'll have to leave,
the nurse says.
Security,
she says over her
shoulder and
to Momma,
you're disturbing the
patients,
then she takes

Momma by the arm.

Momma jerks away.
All the kids in the room stare at her
and then at me.

Momma,
I whisper.
I move near to
Liz, put my hand
on her
used-to-be-shiny
auburn hair. Quick-like
before they pull me away
too.

After all I've done . . .
Momma says.

Come on, let's move on out of here. . . .

Two big guys
come in the room

and go to pull Momma away.

But Momma shakes them
off, walks away
proud, head high.

Hope,
Momma says to me,
get your butt in gear.
We are going.

I pause, unable to make myself
leave my sister.
My feet are stuck
to the black and white
squares of the
floor.

Butter yellow and olive green is good
with me,
I say, trembling,
if you want, Liz.
I look
up into her face
from my squatting position.
But it is like she
is not there.

Liz doesn't say a thing back.
She doesn't even look at me.
She just
sits.

100.

I think we have something here,
Dr. Marino says to
Momma, later that afternoon.

I sit in his office with her.

Momma, tense in her chair,
flutters her hands in the air,
like butterflies maybe.
Or a pale moth.

Can I smoke?
she says.

Dr. Marino gives a
little nod at the ashtray
on the table near Momma's
chair.

Momma lights up.
Her hands shake.

Well,
she says,
after she's blown

smoke out her nose
and let it seep from
her lips,
well, I hope somebody
can tell me something,
because this is costing
me a helluva lotta time.
And time means
money to me.

I look at the doctor.
For a moment I
wish I could take
a drag from Momma's
cigarette,
that's how scared I am.

It's the dreams,
he says.
The crying dreams your daughter keeps
having.

My stomach turns to icy Jell-O.
I feel my guts
shake.

I feel my guts
tremble.

Liz is trying to kill herself
because of dreams?
Momma's voice is high
and quivery.
Jell-O-y sounding
too.

The dreams are Hope's,
Dr. Marino says, and he points
at me.

Now Momma looks
to where I sit
like she is surprised
I'm even
in the room.
She says nothing.
Her cigarette burns.

I hate the smell of
cigarette smoke.
I do.

I think this is the key,
Dr. Marino says.
That Hope has these
dreams of crying.
And now that Lizzie's gone,
the dreams have stopped.

Momma jumps to her feet.

That is it,
she shouts
so loud my ears
hurt.

I jerk in
my chair,
cover
my ears with
my hands.

That's it,
Momma shouts
again.
Now you're trying to drag me
and Hope into this.

Please remain calm,
the doctor says.

But Momma will have none of that.

She grabs me by the arm,
pinching,
and
tugs me to my feet.

Understand this, Dr. Marino,
she says.
I'll have Liz-baby
out of this hospital before you can
count to five.
You hear me?

Mrs. Chapman,
he says,
please have a seat.
I think we have a major
breakthrough here.

Dr. Marino stands too.
He reaches out to Momma,

but she slaps at his hand.
Ashes fall to the carpet in a hunk.
The whole room
feels hot,
tips.
Momma's hand squeezes,
bruises.

I'll step on
those ashes,
I think,
if they set the rug
on fire.

But the fire
is Momma.

I'm getting Lizzie out of here.
Momma's voice is so loud
it makes my ears hurt.
You're filling her head
with stuff and now you're
filling Hope's head with
dreams. I will not allow it.
Get me whatever papers

I need to sign. Now.

Your daughter is in no condition . . .
the doctor says.

Don't you hear me?
Don't you hear me?
I will call the police.
The police.
Do you hear me?

Dr. Marino opens the door
to his office.
The secretary looks at us,
wide-eyed,
half standing
half sitting,
hand on the phone.

Momma keeps that tight
hold on my arm
and I say nothing.
I pretend that this
isn't happening
to me.

Or Lizzie.

But,
the thing is,
I saw her
change.
Right before my eyes.
A magic
trick.
My Lizzie,
changed
from who
she was to who
she isn't.

She's not ready to go home....
He tries to say more.

I don't care what you think,
Momma says.
She's in Dr. Marino's face now.
I ... want ... my ... baby.

Dr. Marino says,
We can talk about this

another day.

At first I think,
He's
scared of Momma,
like I am.
But then I see
he's mad.
Mad!
There's anger in his
face
the way his jaw
works at the words,
the way he clenches
his hands.

We can talk about it
later, nothing,
Momma shouts.

Dr. Marino fills the doorway
then.

You may not
speak

to me that way,
Mrs. Chapman,
he says.

And you may *not*
have your daughter.
She won't be
going anywhere.

Momma is in his face
and he is in hers.

They stand there,
toe-to-toe
chin-to-chin.

We'll see about that,
Momma says.
And then we are gone.
Momma pulling me
along
holding on to me
like Liz held that
belt.

101.

Worse than Momma's screaming
at Dr. Marino
is her silence as
we drive home.

She's
planning
something.

102.

Momma has sent me away.
She's visiting with someone
at the house. Earning
extra money.

I think I'll go to Mari's,
I say,
when she tells me
she has a friend coming over.
But I know as I say
the words I'm lying.

Don't come back
until his car is gone,
Momma says
and she looks up the driveway,
watching.
She is so nervous.

My heart thumps shallow beats
as I wander, casual-like,
to my room.
I remember the belt Liz carved
my initials on, *HKC*, in three places.

I glance
around and make a leap
toward Lizzie's bed,
and all in one move,
grab the diary and tuck it away
in the waistband
of my shorts,
pull my shirt over,
and it's
hidden.

I run past Momma
standing in the
living room, staring at
herself in the
mirror,
then I am out of the door,
hollering,
See you,
to my mother who doesn't even
answer.
Up the driveway I go,
out onto the road,
barefoot.
I leave prints behind in the sand.

I think,
Where now?
Where is safe
now?

103.

Mari's is a
no.
The library is so far from here.
And school is too.
But the river.
The river is nearby.
It won't take me long to get there.

So that's where I go,
jogging as much of the way
as I can.
Fear moves me
and the diary moves
trying to work free
of my waistband
and I wonder why I should be
afraid.

But I am.
I saw Momma.
Lizzie.
Dr. Marino.
And I am scared.

The sun's hot and the air,

heavy.
If I am lucky it'll rain today,
maybe even while I'm out,
thin the air some,
wash this fear
away from
me.

I get to the river and
scramble down the bank.
I smell the spiciness of the weeds
and the sandiness of the shore. I
can even smell the sun.
I find a place to sit,
a place that's far from the road
but still in a clearing. No
need in surprising a nest of snakes.

No need in getting surprised myself.

For the longest time I sit still,
the book resting on my lap.

I sit there
hoping

that whatever is bothering
my sister so bad
has been written in these pages.

And hoping,
just as hard,
that it has not.

104.

Shhh, don't cry.

Momma.

Low voices.
So low, I dream them.

Shhh, don't cry.
Not a sound now.

Mama she say, Shh.
She say, Shhh.
She say, Quiet, baby.

No, no, no.
Not a sound now.
My dream cries on.
Cries me to deeper sleep.

105.

At first there is nothing
in the diary.
Just jibber-jabber.
Stuff about school.
About Amanda and Cheri.
Talk about guys they
think are cute.
Why she doesn't
love her English class
but does love geometry.

I remember my sister before.
It's not that long ago.
The date tells me less
than six months ago
Lizzie was still Lizzie.

Still seeing her friends.
Not crying at night,
no need for a dog
or a sister
to stay close by.

What changed?
I squeeze my eyes shut

a moment.
What
did
Momma
do?

I know it was Momma.
Somehow
it was
Momma.

Guilt creeps up my throat,
making a bad taste
come into my mouth.
I close the diary and look at the sky.

A cloud billows there.
It reminds me
of melted marshmallow,
only whiter.
The sky is so blue
it hurts my eyes.

Dr. Marino,
I say.

You are wrong.
There's nothing here.

My hands shake
as I open the diary again.
I read on.

Same old stuff:
boys
lunch
friends
embarrassing things at school
favorite books
me
lots of me
and how Lizzie
is glad we
are sisters.

I let out a sigh.
He's wrong,
I say in the breeze.

And then
there

it
is.

Slow words,
crawling on the page.

March 23—

I have to write this.

I don't want to.

I don't want to do this.

Any of it.

Thurs—

Too dirty to write

Fri—

Floyd Brackney

back two days in a row.

Good money, Momma says.

I hurt, not just down there,

but everywhere.

He's repeat business

that I do not want.

My face has gone to
ice.
Repeat business?
I say
and look
at the marshmallow cloud.

Momma has said that,
Repeat business,
to me
about people who are visiting *her*.

About
men

who are visiting
her.

My head feels like concrete.
I look up from the page.
My mouth is so dry
I cannot swallow.

The dream-crying sits on the
edge of my mind,
dangling its feet into my memory.

I read again.

Another day—

Today, there was a new man.

Momma told me to look at him.

His belly was fat

and he hurt me.

Momma sat in a corner chair

and watched it all.

I cry, but no one hears

me.

No one.

Not even Hope.

I squeeze my eyes shut again.
Open them.

The crying?
The dream crying?
Waitwaitwaitwaitwait.
My hands tremble
as I turn the page
back, looking.

Not even a month
has passed for my sister,
the writer.
She must be making up these words.
I cannot believe . . .

but there are pictures,
folded up small,
tucked in the pages.

At first I cannot figure
what the one is,
I have never seen anything
like this before.
And then, as I look closer, I realize . . .

A man ready to have sex.
I'm not sure how I know,
I just do.

She's drawn
only a stick figure man,
except for that part of his body
that has been erased a few times
and drawn over and over
then *x*'d out.

This cannot be right,
what I am thinking
cannot be right.
I can't quite see

it straight.

Dear God.
Dear Jesus.
Jesus God.
Please, God.

Where are You?

My concrete head pounds.
My eyes feel dried out,
like maybe I have left them
open too long.
How long have I been
sitting here anyway?
I look out at the river
and now my eyes burn.
Nothing is pretty here anymore.
And that cloud
hasn't even moved.

Another day.

Why so much?

I can't tell Hope.

Momma says I can't

or she'll make her help,

make her do this too.

Another day.

I can't be friends

with Cheri anymore

or Amanda.

They might look at me and know.

They might see what is gone from me.

They might see how I have changed

if I open

my mouth to them.

I can only glance at the words.
They make me sick.
My mouth is too dry now.
A glimpse at a time,
that is all I can stand.
And even that tears me up.
A glimpse is all I can stand.

I turn pages so slow a snail could go
faster.

When he got on me . . .

Momma said, Kiss him. Use your tongue. . . .

She watched from the corner. . . .

I can't sleep.

I'm too scared to sleep.

And I can't stop the crying

when it comes.

I'm lost.

Not me anymore.

Momma says

she will make

Hope do this.

But I won't let that happen.

Never!

I keep seeing a picture,
another picture that's a face,
with tears that drip down both
cheeks
and to the bottom
of the page.

I'm surprised when a tear
of my own splats on the face,
the face that is so Lizzie,
this self-portrait,

and then I'm crying.

I toss the diary away from me
and it lands in the river with a slap.

I feel a scream
building up inside,
but what I do is throw up.

Because I *have* known.
I have had the dreams.
The crying was real.
My crying sister,
my Lizzie.
Protecting me.

Taking care of
me.

Mama she say, Shh.
She say, Shhh.
She say, Quiet, baby.

106.

Last summer,
Lizzie and me
went to a different place
on the river.

Not where we saw the snakes with
Momma,
not where I go with Mari.
It was backwoods more.

Momma had sent us both away,
so we packed up a lunch
and hiked out to the water.
Then, by accident, walked to this place.

It was a cross,
where two rivers met
and the small one spilled into the larger.
A shallow pool had formed
and when we found it,
hiking along like there was only today,
neither one of us said a word for a
moment.

Then I said,

I'm taking me a dip.

Right that second
I stripped down to my
underwear even though
the elastic on one
leg was half stitched on.

Liz said,
Somebody might be watching.

Let 'em watch,
I said
and plunged into the water.

It was cool
and beneath my feet
the bottom slipped away
till I paddled to stay afloat.

There could be snakes,
Liz said, taking off
her clothes
too.

Let 'em come.

There could be 'gators.

Let 'em show up.

Liz laughed a big ol' belly laugh.

And I laughed too,
water sweeping in my mouth a bit,
but not so much I couldn't
spit it out and be happy along
with my sister.

Then she was in the water beside me.

And any of those things—
the watcher,
the snake,
or the killer alligator—

would have been better
than what I found out
today.

107.

I can't go home,
not now that I know.

I'm too sick.
So I sit out on the river
and remember.

Me and Lizzie singing harmony.
Me and Lizzie riding the school bus
together.
Me and Lizzie giggling in the evening
before the night fell like a dark blanket
and Lizzie's smile faded.

I remember the one time
when I hadn't been at Mari's
house that long and Liz called.

This was
before I found her
with the
gun.

Hey, Hope,
she said,

how long do you think
till you're home?
Momma wants to know.

Her voice was soft and
almost worried sounding.
Protecting me.
Taking care of me.

A couple of hours,
I said.
We're planning a picnic.
You wanna come?

Liz was silent a moment,
then she whispered,
I better not. I gotta
stay here.
And then she said,
Are you sure it has to be so long?

Does Momma want me back sooner?
Again
Liz took a second to answer.

No,
she said.
She won't care how long you're gone.

Well, I'll see you later,
I said
and went to hang up the phone.

Hope?
Lizzie said.
I love you.

Hey, Hope,
Mari said.
Let's get going. Looks like rain.

I'm coming,
I said to Mari
and then to Liz,
Sure you don't want to come?

Can't,
she said.

I'll make it quick.

I'll try to get home sooner.
I felt surprised
I said those words.
I wanted to be a little free,
rain or not.
A picnic would be fun,
especially since Mari
had chosen to pack the lunch.
Her momma always bought
things my momma
wouldn't think to,
like Twinkies and Cheetos.

If Liz hadn't sounded so sad,
I wouldn't have given
our afternoon adventure
a second thought.

But I said to her,
Liz, I'll only be gone awhile.
Just long enough to bike
out to the river,
have a picnic,
and come back home.
No playing around.

How's that?
She let out a sigh, and said,
That's good, Hope.
That's real good.

Her voice, though,
it was different.
I mean,
it wasn't happy
like the words were.
It was like
she was saying,
Go, don't go.
Go, don't go.

My memories cause my
throat to close up now.

The diary is caught
in weeds, right
there at the lip of
the river.

I need that thing
away

from me where the words
and pictures won't bite
at my heart.

All at once the tears I
didn't cry when Lizzie
went into the hospital
pour out right then,
on that riverbank.

I cry like someone I
love has died. I cry
with big gasping sobs,
sobs that make
my whole body shake from pain.

When I can't cry anymore,
I gather my courage
and go home to see
my momma.

108.

Where have you been?
Momma says.

It's been hours since I left.

At first
I don't say anything.
This whole way from
the river I've been
thinking that I can say
something to Momma,
say something about Liz
and the diary
and the things that I read.

But when I see her standing
there in the living room,
I feel like I am going
to throw up again.

I asked you, Where have you been?
Momma says.
I wanted to go and
see my Lizzie,
to tell her we're bringing

433

her home Monday,
and you have
made us too late
to do anything.

Momma stretches,
her arms going up
over her head.
Her shirt creeps up a bit
and I see
a line of tanned belly,
her belly ring,
a bit of a new tattoo
down low.
I look away.

Somehow,
when I open my
mouth, words come out.
How could you?
I say.
My voice shakes,
that's true, but I'm
saying something.

In fact,
everything shakes on me.
My guts,
my knees,
my lips.
But I am saying
something.

Momma looks at me,
then goes to close the curtains
on this trailer
the smells of us
living so close.

What the hell
are you talking about?
she says,
her voice careful.

I read the diary,
I say.

Momma's back is to me,
but I see her pause,

almost stumble
in her shutting
out the world from our home.

I read the diary,
I say again,
and this time I'm
really afraid.

Afraid of Momma who isn't
a thing that I thought
she was,
though now that I put my mind to it,
I'm not sure what I believed
about her.

How could you?
I say again.

Momma turns,
starts toward me,
barefoot on the linoleum,
her feet patting out a light sound.
She isn't even close
to me, but still I flinch.

Hope,
she says.
Her voice is soft. Singsongy.
It's not what you think.

I try to make my mouth work.
I am so scared. So scared.
Because she
does not even deny it. She could
deny it.
But she doesn't. She
just says,
It's not what you think.

I can't think.
She's right about that.
The confusing part of thinking.
She's right, I'm thought-less.

Momma watches me.
Does she see me hesitate?
Does she see me falter?

My mouth is open.
No words come out now.

There is
nothing in the air
between us.

Except Lizzie.

Momma starts to turn away
and I see a smile
about to come to her lips.

Not what I think?
I make myself say it.
The words are like cotton.
They puff out
of my mouth.

Momma turns back again,
faces me.
The smile is there.
Your sister said she wanted
to help me make some money,
Momma says.

She takes a quiet step closer.
She holds out her hands, palms up,

like maybe she didn't have
a choice in things.

I back away from her.
We aren't that much apart in size.
In fact, I stand a little taller than her.
I will fight her if I have to.

What you did,
I say,
is all wrong.
At first I am not even
sure she hears me.

What have I done that's so bad?
Momma says.
What, Hope?
I've given you a home.
Made sure you have
food on the table.
Let you go to Mari's.

This is all true.
But there's the diary,
my head says.

And Liz trying to die.
And her being away.

Haven't I done all that
for you?

Yes, Momma,
I say.
But . . .

But what?

Momma is close now.
So close
I could hug her
or slap her.

I squeeze my eyes shut.
Do it,
I think.
Do it.
Say it.

It's all a lie,
I say.

You are all a lie.

Momma doesn't even move.
She just stares at me.
Her mouth falls
open.
And she looks and looks at me.

I touch my fingers
to my lips.

It's not a lie,
Momma says.
It's true, Hope.

For a moment, I almost believe her.
Then I remember the diary.
The words.
My sister.
The ways she's tried to
end
her
life.

Momma takes in a

breath,
rocks back on her heels.

Then she says,
Lizzie owes
me.
And you, Hope.
She owes you, too.

What?
My fingers are
still there, still touching
my lips, but
the word gets past.
What do you mean she owes us?

Momma keeps rocking
and her arms go around
herself.

She owes us for
taking your daddy
from us.

What?

Being sick
that night,
Momma says,
looking up at me,
and I see she believes
what she's saying.
For her being sick
and him going
out
in all that rain
and sliding under
that truck
and not coming back.

She owes us for that.
Taking my man.
And your daddy.

I swallow again and again.
She
was
just
six,
I say.

But Momma is away and thinking
something.
Then she says,

She's in the hospital,
She's safe.
The doctors will help her.
And I promise
I won't let nothing
happen to her again.

We'll bring her here
on Monday and
she'll be safe with us.
Okay? How's that?

I'll make it all better,
Momma says.

Again, I almost believe
until she says,

Now give me that diary.

I wait.

Don't say a thing.
And then, blood pumping,
fear streaking,
eyes dried out from too
much crying.

It's gone,
I say.
The diary is gone.
I threw it in the river.

Momma catches
hold of my arm.

Give me that diary,
she says. Her lips don't move.
You know what kind of trouble
I can get into from that?

I wish I *had* saved it,
I say,
my voice getting louder.
Something grows in me
so big that I think
I will pop with it

if I don't let it out.

But I do.
I holler at Momma,
I wish I had shouted
what I read
to everyone. I wish
everyone in the world
knew how crazy you are.

Momma
squeezes a tight hold on me,
pinching at my arms.
She backs me up,
until I am pinned and pressed
close and
hard and
tight against the wall.

I am not crazy,
she says.
Her teeth are tight when she speaks.
I am *not* crazy.
Don't you ever say that to me again.

I look at my momma
standing there in her
too-tight clothes and smelling
her breath that's like sour beer.

I look at her makeup,
smeared under her eyes,
and her face strained with anger.

I remember how,
when I was little,
I had thought she was pretty.
The prettiest momma in all the world.
Now everything about her is
ugly.

And I wonder,
will I ever feel the same
about her again?

I hate you,
I say.
My voice is low and angry.
I hate you for
what you did to

my sister.

Where is that diary?
Momma says,
bringing her face close to mine,
her words on my skin.
I turn away from her,
then squirm free.

She grabs my hair,
jerking me back.

I swing out at her,
missing.

For a moment I think
she will tear at my skin
with her teeth she's so mad,
but she just shouts,
Where?

I told you,
I shout back.
I told you
I threw it down the river.

I threw it down the river.
It's gone.

I jerk free with a shake
and push her away.

You make me sick,
I say.

I run then,
from her,
from the house.

109.

Me and Lizzie
Me and Lizzie
Me and Lizzie.

Shhh.
Hush, baby,
hush now.

Shhhh.

110.

I stop running
just long enough to grab
the damp diary from the mailbox
where it waits,
hiding.

I tuck it into my shorts
so it can't be seen if
Momma drives past,
looking for me.

Then I start a slow walk
to
Mari's.

Night is a deep dark by now
and the moon
is up good in the sky.

I've been walking
for just a few minutes
when I hear it.

Momma's car
coming in my direction.

With a start I run into a
stand of trees that grows
close to the edge of the road
and throw myself on the ground.

A few moments later
the headlights round the curve and
Momma and the car appear.

Looking.
Looking for me.

Hope,
she calls from the car window.

Hope. Let's go see Lizzie.
Her voice is so different
I almost do not recognize it.

Who is she?
My heart thumps
into the ground
beneath me.

I lie flat,

smelling the sand and
dead leaves under me.

Mosquitoes start biting
but I don't move,
just watch Momma drive
down the road going
slower than I can walk.

She can hear my heart,
I think.
It pounds so
that it seems to echo
into the earth.

Hope, I know you can hear me,
she says.
Come on, baby.
Get in the car.
I'll make you safe and Lizzie
safe too.
Nothing to worry about.

The car stops a few feet ahead of
where I am.

I watch the light in Momma's
car come on.
I watch as she gets out.
She walks to the far side of
the street, talking the whole time.

I lose her sound for a moment.
Blood pounds in my ears.
I think I might vomit again.

Then,
Hope, I know you're here,
Momma says.
I know you're here.
Let's go on home together.
Come on, baby.

I start to cry, but
I don't move at all.
Not at all.
And I don't
make a sound.
Not one.
I've even stopped
breathing.

Just let those tears slide down
my face
and drip into
the sand.

Momma steps into the
grass not far from me.
You want me to leave her in the
hospital?
Momma says.
Just you and me take off?

The tears drip in the leaves.

We can go somewhere
no one knows us.
Just you
and
me.

I could do it,
I think.

I could go back with her.
Just me and Momma.

Not anyone would know
the truth.
No one but me.
And Lizzie.

And Momma.

She's quiet.
When she speaks again
her voice sounds even less
like her.

I will find you, she says.
And no one will ever know
what happened.

In slow motion
Momma turns and walks back to the
car.

Then she's gone,
slow,
up the road,
slow,
out of sight,

slow,
around the next bend.

I keep lying still,
not moving,
just waiting.

Just waiting.

Then I'm off to Mari's house,
again,
running,
and every once in a while
I hear Momma, driving around.

Looking for me.

111.

I need to speak to Dr. Kyle Marino,
I whisper into the phone,
hidden in Mari's closet.
I know it's late, but he told me to call
him.

There is a shuffling noise
and I hear the woman
say,
Some girl, Kyle.
I really wish you wouldn't
give out our home number.

My face turns red.

Just think of Lizzie,
I say to myself.

Mari, guarding her closet door,
says,
Did you get him, Hope?
Are you talking
to him?
Her voice is strained.

Not yet,
I say.

A moment passes.

This is Dr. Marino.
His voice is deeper
than in the daytime.

And me?
I can't say anything.

Hello?

Umm,
I manage to get that
bit of a sound out.

Yes, I'm here,
he says.
Can I help you?

I hope so,
I whisper.

My heart pounds.
If Momma finds out.
If she knew about that diary.

Who is this?
Dr. Marino says.

My tears crack wide open
again and I am crying
without saying
a word.

Before I could not cry.
Now, maybe,
I'll never stop.

Lizzie,
I say at last.

Elizabeth Chapman?
he says.

My sister,
I say.

Hope?
Mari's voice is soft at the crack
of the closet door.
Are you okay?

I shake my head no.

The pain in my heart is
so deep I don't think I
can take a full breath.

Hope?
Dr. Marino says,
his voice as soft as Mari's.
What do you
have for me?

Lizzie
alone
in the hospital,
painting my belt,
waiting at home
while I play with my friends.

Watching
out
for
me.

This is . . .
I say.

You know what kind
of trouble I can get into
from that?

This is . . .
I say again.

Tell him,
Mari says.
Tell him, Hope.

Oh Jesus,
dear Jesus,
I say.

In my head
I see Lizzie.

Hope,
I love you.

How could I do it?
I say to Dr. Marino.
How could I leave her?

There are no words
for the sickness that fills my body.

Yes, go ahead, I'm listening,
the doctor says.

Dear Jesus.
Dear Jesus.

You can do it, Hope,
Mari says.
Tell him.

I can't say it,
I say to Mari,
who knows what the diary says
too.

Tell him who you are,
she says.

Hope?
Dr. Marino says.

Those weren't crying dreams,
I say.

I suck in a deep breath of air.
I can smell the leather
of Mari's shoes.

They were real.
My voice is a whisper again.

Hope, I'm listening.

I hurt not just down there.
Can't you please
stay with me, Hope?
Hope?

My sister,
my sister.

Tell for your best sister.

I squish my eyes closed
and take in another deep breath.

Dr. Marino is quiet.

You can do it,
Mari says.

Again I gulp in air.

I found the diary,
I say.
The one you wanted that
Lizzie wrote.
I found the diary and I
know what's been
happening with my
sister.

112.

Mari
waits for me.

I put the phone
in the cradle,
squeeze my eyes shut, and
wait
because
I have to.

The door
opens
without a sound.

Leave me just one
more minute,
I say,
not looking up
because it feels
like a rock has settled on
my shoulders.

Momma says,
Get the hell

out of those shoes
and let's get going.

What?
I say.

For a moment
I cannot breathe.
It's like she has
her hand around my throat
though all Momma
does is look down at
where I am.

Then she reaches for me
and behind Momma
is Mari
and her mother
and her father
and even Mattie,
all surprised
with looking.

Come with me,

Momma says,
reaching.

No,
I say and
I scoot back into the
belly of this closet,
away from Momma
who keeps coming
with an arm
that seems way too long.

We're leaving,
she says
between her teeth.
We're leaving here now.

She has my arm then.
Momma pulls me to my feet
and her fingers are
tight
tight
tight.

I'm not going,

I want to say,
but the words will not come
out of my mouth.

Momma is close then,
close to my face,
and I can smell something
that makes my stomach
turn, though I
am not sure what
it is.

Go on now, Hope,
Mari's momma says.
Go on with
your mother.

No,
says Mari,
and she
reaches for my
other arm.
She can't go
with her.
She's staying here

with me.

Marianna!
Mari's father says,
and he sounds
surprised.

But Momma
doesn't seem to
hear any of that.

Momma just bores holes
into my skin with
a look that could fry flesh.

You think I got time,
she says,
to mess with you?

She leans into my face
and Mari tries to
pull me away
but Momma is lots stronger.

I don't have time for any

470

of this,
she says.
I'm going.

And Momma looks at me again.
I got places to go,
she says.

And I see so much
in that look.
Hear so much in that voice.

That she did hurt my sister.
That she doesn't care about
Liz
or me,
for that matter.
And that life with her
will never
change.

We stare at each other.
The room is more than quiet,
like we have all died
or are getting ready to.

I told him,
I whisper.
I told him what I read,
I say louder.
They know now,
I say.
They know what
you did to
my Liz.

I am not going with you.
Now my voice is loud
enough that everyone can hear
and Mari's mom says,
Hope?
And Mari says,
Mom, don't.

Momma lets loose of
my arm.

You told them?
she says.

My eyes fill up with tears.

I'm not sure
if I can live with my
decision.

But I cannot forget
Liz,
my sister Liz,
and those words
on wrinkled diary pages.

I stare back at Momma.

She shrugs.
No one will believe you,
you little slut,
she says.
She pushes past
everyone.
I'll see my own way out.

And then she's gone.

113.

I don't see Momma
again.
For three weeks, I wait,
thinking maybe she
will come back.

But she doesn't.

First, I tell Mari
Momma's gone,
then I go and visit
Miss Freeman
who folds me into her
body and
says,
You can stay right here, honey.

Maybe,
I say,
maybe I can help
you at the store.
I'm good with adding.
Good with money.

Maybe you can,
she says.

Last thing?
I call Dr. Marino
one more
time.

114.

The state
says Temporary Custody
with Miss Freeman,
just for a little while,
and then I can
stay
with my grandmother,
if I want.
If she wants too.

But I don't know
my father's mother
that well.

I want to stay here,
I tell the judge.
Here with Miss Freeman,
so I can help
her with her store
and so I can be close to Mari
and so I can see Alex.

Temporary Custody,
he says,

but I can tell he
hears what I say.

We'll see how it
works out,
he says.

115.

I am mixed up inside
and bothered
that I miss my mother
who is gone
but Dr. Marino says
he can help me
work through it all
if I want.

If *I* want.

And I do. To work
it out,
figure why it was Lizzie
and not me
with those men.
And how things
might have been different
if Daddy
hadn't died
that night.

This is going to take a while,
I say
to Dr. Marino.

I got lots of questions.

And he just nods.

116.

It feels like
it has been months,
years,
eons
since I've seen
Liz.

It's time to go to the hospital,
and Mari's grandmother
drives me and Mari
and we're safe
because the lights
don't need to be on.
We're going in the
middle of the afternoon.

Going to see my
Liz.

At last we're there,
driving closer and closer
to the hospital
and my sister.

My heart,

it thumps, hard,
like it has a
mind of its own.

When we park,
I hurry ahead of my friend,
hurry ahead of her grandmother,
hurry ahead
till I am
out of the Florida sun
and in the coolness of the
hospital.

Lizzie's doing crafts,
the nurse at the desk says.
Come this way.

I know the way,
I say.
Please tell my friends.
Please,
I say,
let them know
where we are.

I point to Mari who
walks fast, her grandmother
following behind, and
I feel the beginning of a rose
start in my heart
that thumps so hard
it almost hurts.

I'm off,
toward the
Arts and Crafts room,
racing there.
Till I get
to the doorway.

I stand
watching
Lizzie.

She works on a pot,
coiling clay into a
snakelike thing.

I watch her, thin and timid,

but
there ...

I see it ...
I see the glimmer of a smile.

The rose in my heart starts to unfold.

Liz,
I say
and my voice is a whisper,
and thin like a glimpse,
but it travels over to her
and she looks up at me
and smiles
like I hold a camera
and asked her to
pose.
She smiles
like I take a picture,
a picture I
can remember later,
a picture I could tuck
in the box under Momma's

bed,
if it was real.

Hope,
she says. And then,
Look what I have for you.
She pulls out the belt,
dotted butter yellow
and
olive green.

It dangles behind her,
like a dog pulled along might,
and the blossom in my
heart is full bloom now.

I close my eyes,
close my eyes to tears,
and walk in to meet
my sister,
Liz.

THE END

ACKNOWLEDGMENTS

The truth about a book is that it starts from a seed and grows, if you're lucky, into a tree. And there are lots of people who help cultivate the ground around that tree. My writing life is no different. There are many who inspire, boost, and support.

First, I want to thank my agent, Stephen Fraser. Steve took me on as a client a few years back with a dark novel then called *A Glimpse Is All I Can Stand*. He knows the business of books, has soothed my bruised ego countless times, and even brought me flowers to brighten my hotel room. He is not only my agent, but a dear friend. When I suggested the wonderful Alexandra Penfold as a possible editor for *Glimpse* he agreed whole-heartedly. Alexandra is wonderful to work with and helped me extensively, making the book work better and more smoothly. Having an editor who wants you to succeed makes the revision process all that more exciting. A big thank-you, too, to Lizzy Bromley who created the gorgeous cover.

I want to say a special thank-you to Phyllis Reynolds Naylor who, for years, has helped writers achieve their dreams. A version of this novel won The PEN/Phyllis Naylor Working Writer Fellowship. Hugs and thanks to committee members Lucy Frank, Patricia Reilly Giff, and Ann M. Martin for choosing my novel out of so many that also deserved the honor. I cannot express how much this award boosted my confidence as a writer. As well, many thanks to Nick Burd, Literary Awards Program Manager at the PEN American Center, and the PEN staff for making my time in New York lovely. I smile still, remembering those few days with you all.

I was lucky enough to attend Vermont College for two years and had the first twenty pages of this book workshopped by an amazing group of writers. My class leaders were Marion Dane Bauer and Martine Leavitt, whose careful criticism made me believe I could keep working on a book that I had spent nearly half a decade revising.

A special thank-you to Cheri Earl, Rick Walton, John Bennion, Ann Dee Ellis, Chris Crowe, and Lu Ann Staheli. These writers are good friends with the ability to give smart critique.

Finally, and mostly, a thank-you to all my daughters—Elise, Laura, Kyra, Caitlynne, and Carolina. You have always believed in me even in the dark times (and there have been plenty). Thank you for having faith in a flawed parent. I adore you all.